D1707778

About the Author

Goretti Kyomuhendo was the first female Ugandan writer to be invited to the International Writing Program at the University of Iowa - USA in 1997. Subsequently, she became an honorary fellow in creative writing. Her first novel, *The First Daughter* by **Fountain Publishers** (1996), enjoyed immense popularity both in her home country Uganda, and outside. She has also written for children: *Different Worlds,* by **The Monitor Publications** (1997) and has finished her third novel, *Whispers from Vera.*
Kyomuhendo presently works with FEMRITE as its Co-ordinator.

For Jennifer

In the spirit of togetherness

Goretti
July 2002
Kampala

Secrets no More

Goretti Kyomuhendo

FEMRITE Publications
KAMPALA

FEMRITE Publications
P.O. Box 705
KAMPALA, Uganda
Tel:543943

©Goretti Kyomuhendo 1999

First Published 1999
Second Edition 2001

All rights reserved. The text of this publication or any part there-of may not be reproduced or transmitted in any form or by any means, electronic or mechanical, including photocopying, recording, storage in an information retrieval system now known or hereafter invented, without the written permission of the Publisher.

Printed in Uganda by The New Vision

ISBN 9970 90 10 5 2

To the memory of my late sister, Joy,
For all that she did for me, for us.

CONTENTS

PROLOGUE

PART ONE..   1

PART TWO   83

PART THREE   124

GLOSSARY   176

PROLOGUE

"You have every reason to be proud," Mukundane whispered in the ears of the baby lying asleep in her arms. "You are light-skinned and you will be tall and elegant. Your speech," Mukundane continued, "will be cultured, smooth, not like *abaswa.*"

The baby opened her eyes; they were big and crystal clear. She smiled at her mother and gurgled happily.

"Yes, my princess? I can see you are awake now and I know you understand what I am telling you," Mukundane said excitedly.

"No, *Mabuja,* she cannot understand what you are telling her. She is only six months old," Chantal, who was standing behind her mistress, reprimanded her gently.

"You ought to be proud of your forefathers too," Mukundane continued talking to the baby as if she had not heard Chantal's reprimand. "They trace their roots to the Abyssinian mountains in Ethiopia, that land of the most beautiful and courageous people in Africa. They repulsed European rule, you know."

"*Mabuja,* don't overload the little one's mind with such strong words!" Chantal said sternly. "Here, she is asleep now, let me take her to bed," Chantal persuaded her mistress.

"Your forefathers, they were cattle keepers too," Mukundane continued in a husky voice, her eyes glistening with unshed tears. She was now talking more to herself than to the baby. "They were the *abaami* of this land. They were learned and they had power."

"Oh *Mabuja, "*Chantal whispered gently to her mistress, "please do not torment yourself so! You have told me all this a thousand times before."

Chantal was crying with her mistress. She came and sat beside her, one arm slung over her shoulders in a comforting gesture. After a while Mukundane's sobs subsided and Chantal quietly took the baby from her arms.

PART ONE

Chapter One

When Chantal first came to work for the Bizimana family, they had just got married. Bizimana was ten years older than his wife but that was no cause for alarm; women aged much faster than men, and within a short time the two would begin to look the same age. Nor did the fact that Bizimana was a Hutu, while Mukundane, his wife was a Tutsi. Hutu men occasionally married Tutsi women, though the latter were called derogatory names like *Inyenzikazi* or *Maguruyasarwaya*.

Mukundane had grown up with a kind Hutu family which had adopted her at the age of nine after her parents' massacre in the 1959 uprisings. Mukundane had been an only child and had not got a chance to interact much with her other relatives who now lived in Uganda as refugees. The Hutu family had been good to her.

"We are only reciprocating your late parents' good deeds. They were good neighbours to us long before you were born," they would say to her.

Mukundane often recounted the horrors she had witnessed as a child during the 1959 civil war to Chantal who was both her companion and live-in maid.

"The Hutu took up arms and overthrew the Tutsi monarch. The Tutsi, my parents included, died in big numbers. Others flew to USA and Canada. I survived because the Hutu never killed the children. When I went to school, I learnt more about our country's history. Our history teacher told us that in 1969, Rwanda was declared a republic and Kayibanda was named as its first president. People jubilated, monarchies had been abolished forever. But four years later, Kayibanda was overthrown by his Army Chief-of -Staff, Habyarimana. Things changed; a one party system was established..."

Mukundane never tired of telling this story. She would tell it again and again. At other times, Chantal would reprimand her mistress sternly or simply refuse to listen. After reminiscing, Mukundane would break into uncontrollable sobs. Crying for her dead parents and displaced relatives. Chantal was always there to wipe away her tears, to console and comfort her.

"Mabuja," she would whisper in her ear, talking soothingly as one would to a hurt child. "You did not even know them. Besides, they must be happy where they are."

"They are still my family, and I miss them."

"And you got other parents who loved you so much."

"Yes...yes, and they were killed too because they were not Hutu from the South."

At such times, Chantal would see no point in arguing further with her mistress and she would quietly walk away.

Her husband had been desperate to make her happy. He always tried to draw her out in conversation but she always kept mum, never explaining her source of unhappiness. Maybe it was because of their ethnic differences, maybe it was the difference in their age, or level of education, maybe...he wished she could open up to him. That was when the idea of getting her a companion, one she would feel free to confide in, had occurred to him. He remembered the day he had first met Chantal.

That day, a woman who had refused to participate in *Umuganda* had been brought to him. *Umuganda* was a scheme where all adults were supposed to give a day of free community work each week. It was detested by the people and their participation was ensured by threats. The penalty for evading *Umuganda* was imprisonment.

"Nyakubahwa, this woman said she is your relative and asked to speak to you before we take her to jail," the policeman who had arrested the woman said.

"I have never seen her in my life," Bizimana said, surprised. "Take her away."

"No sir, please let me explain: it's not that I don't want to work, but I have two small children and my husband died last year. I have no one to look after them. I have to fend for them," the woman cried hysterically.

"I said take this woman away!" Bizimana shouted. He felt anger rise to his head. He hated people who tried to frustrate government's policies. Ever since he had become a Minister of Social Works and Rehabilitation a year ago, he had tried his best to implement government policies and execute them to perfection. The fact that he was a Hutu originating from the south did not make matters easy for him. They were considered less of supporters of the government and were always being watched.

The ministerial post, though, had come with benefits: a beautiful mansion in the exclusive residential area of Remera, a luxurious car and membership to the exclusive Kiyovu Club.

The woman was on her knees, begging him still.

"Sir, please have mercy, if not on me, then on those two innocent souls - my babies; they will starve if I'm arrested." Tears were rolling down her cheeks and she looked up at the Minister with eyes full of fright .

Bizimana looked at the woman for a long time. He wondered what had prompted her to come to him. Was she a distant relative of his or had she simply expected him to have mercy on her?

"Woman, don't you see how *Umuganda* has benefited you, the local people? Look at those anti-erosion ditches the people dig," one of the policemen said to the woman.

"Or the health centres and schools constructed under *Umuganda* scheme?" another policeman chipped in. "If you don't build more health centres, those small ones you so love will actually die."

"Please, God, no!" the woman wailed.

Bizimana looked at the woman again. Tears were still rolling down her cheeks. There was something in her eyes and voice which captured his attention. Was it the sincerity behind those frightened eyes or the love in her tone whenever she mentioned her babies?

"Nyakubahwa, this woman is only playing games with us. Let's take her away," one of the policemen began to say but Bizimana cut him off.

"Leave her to me for a moment," he told the policemen. When the policemen left, he turned to the woman.

"What is your name?"

"Nyirabagenzi Chantal."

"Where do you come from?"

"Gisenyi."

3

This raised Bizimana's eyebrows. "Are you a distant relative of mine?"

"No," Chantal answered.

Bizimana was silent for a moment. "And your children, how old are they?"

"I have no children," Chantal answered flatly. "I lied, I hate *Umuganda,*" she continued indignantly.

Bizimana was speechless. He stared at her and Chantal stared back at him without any remorse.

He moved out of the office and called the two policemen who were standing on the veranda. They were in the office in an instant and one of them was brandishing handcuffs. Chantal's eyes fell on the handcuffs and she squirmed in fear.

"Sir, oh please don't let them take me away, I could work for you...for your wife. I could be her...maid...her companion." She was speaking inanely, but the word 'companion' captured Bizimana's attention. That is exactly what his wife needed, a companion to talk to, confide in. This woman looked forty or so...maybe.

"Are you sure you can make a good companion for my wife?" he asked her with doubt.

"Yes, sir, that has always been my job," Chantal answered promptly.

"But you are a liar! How do I know you are not lying again?" Bizimana asked her putting steel in his voice.

"You could crosscheck my background, sir. I lied because I wanted an audience with you," Chantal said convincingly.

"I don't buy that," Bizimana said, shaking his head. "I can't trust you with my wife. Take her away," he said turning to the policemen. "She is a defaulter and you know where she belongs."

Chantal was dragged from the Minister's office amidst protests; she was crying hysterically, calling out the Minister's name and imploring him to have mercy on her.

When Bizimana went home that evening, he told his wife about the strange woman who had been brought to his office. Mukundane was equally puzzled.

"Why do you think she came to you?" she asked her husband.

"I'm not sure, but I suspect that she knows me from my rural home, and probably-"

"She thought you'd be sympathetic?"

"No, she could have heard from someone that I was looking around for...a...companion for you."

4

"Me? Who says I need a companion?" his wife asked furiously.

"Well, I just thought that, maybe you are lonely, and-"

"I don't need any whatever you call her!" she snapped.

Bizimana kept quiet, not knowing what to say. He wished he had not talked about it to anyone.

"Did she mention it?" his wife surprised him by asking.

"Mention what?"

"Well, that she wanted to be my..."

"Yes, she did," Bizimana answered wearily. "But don't break your back about it. I wouldn't trust her any more than I would a thief." He smiled at her reassuringly.

"Yes, I understand, but I wonder why she would risk being thrown in prison in case you refused to buy her story. Like you just did," his wife reasoned.

"Well?"

"She sounds helpless, desperate, like one would in a foreign country. Lost, homeless, unwanted." Tears were beginning to form in her eyes and she had a far away look.

He detected the signs. He knew his wife was about to lapse into one of her sad moods. He wished he had not talked about the strange woman.

"What do you want me to do?" he asked exasperated.

"Maybe...you could...we could...give her a chance." She was now crying openly.

"All right," he said curtly. "I will talk to her again tomorrow."

The following day he sent for the woman and she was again brought to his office. She was haggard. Bizimana felt some compassion for her. He had checked her out thoroughly:

Family: deceased.

Children: none

Former employee: a French family which had gone back to France a year ago but had left her a small fortune because of her dedication.

Experience: eleven years.

He was satisfied.

He told her that he and his wife had agreed to hire her but she would first undergo a three months' probation after which she would keep the job permanently if they were satsified. Chantal took the good news calmly and Bizimana felt a tinge of disappointment. As he gave her a list of what was expected of her, she kept on nodding.

"Do you understand?" he asked irritably.

Chantal looked at her new master for a moment before replying, "I understand, sir."

But that happened many years ago. Chantal had played her role to perfection.

But still his wife was not happy. Now she was becoming even more disconsolate because of her failure to conceive. Bizimana had tried to reassure her. Two years was too short a time to begin worrying but she refused to believe him, saying that it was her fault because she was not woman enough to give her husband children. But Bizimana knew from the doctor's report that there was nothing wrong with her and it was only a matter of time before she conceived.

***

Mukundane still had not conceived three years after their wedding. The doctors said there was nothing seriously wrong with her. "She is not relaxed," one doctor, after another said. "She is only tensed up and over-burdens her mind with worries."

"*Mabuja,* please stop worrying. Everything will be all right. You will see, by this time next year, you will be holding a baby in your arms," Chantal would assure her.

One year turned into another and still Mukundane had no baby to hold in her arms.

Her mind often drifted off and she found herself thinking of the political unrest in the country.

"Chantal, I don't know what will happen. I am torn apart. Don't you hear these things being said on the radio?"

"Which things, *Mabuja?"* Chantal would ask, feigning ignorance. She knew very well what her mistress was talking about. It was becoming her favourite conversation.

"They say people from my ethnic group are being harassed in the countries they live in as refugees. Some are huddled in camps."

"I know, *Mabuja,* but...really..."

"It is not only that, the radio says that all the Tutsi now want to come back to their homeland. And...that if they come, they will kill all the Hutu people in the government...and my husband. I'm afraid for him!"

"I cry with you, *Mabuja.* I know you must be hurting. But as a good wife, you also know what is expected of you. You must give your husband an heir."

With that, Mukundane would become pensive. She still believed that

6

it was her fault that she could not conceive.

***

Meanwhile, some of the Tutsi refugees, especially those living in Uganda had been integrated into the civil society and were slowly losing their identity. Yet the Rwandan government was adamant about their return to their homeland, claiming that the country was too small to accommodate them. It was around that time that the Tutsi refugees formed the Rwandese Alliance for National Unity (RANU) which became the official Rwandan opposition in the diaspora. Attacks on the government began. In return, the Hutu killed some of the Tutsi families still living in Rwanda.

Chapter Two

Marina, Mukundane's first child was born in 1979. She was a tiny pretty child and Chantal took to her immediately. Mukundane was very possessive of her daughter and only referred to her as *Mwamikazi*, meaning "Princess."

"We must teach her everything! Everything, Chantal, you hear?" Mukundane would say, her eyes sparkling with excitement.

"Yes, *Mabuja*. After all, she deserves it."

"She must not miss what I missed after my parents were killed. She must grow up like a true princess."

"Of course, *Mabuja*," Chantal answered promptly. She understood her mistress' need to give her daughter the very best out of life. After all, her husband was a very wealthy man and it had taken her many years before holding a baby in her arms.

Marina was very precious to both parents. And so by the time she was five years, a governess had been hired to give her lessons in swimming, playing the piano and dancing ballet.

Marina was natural at everything she did. She was elegant and walked with grace. The title of 'princess' could not have befitted her more.

Bizimana too adored his beautiful daughter. Unfortunately, the political unrest in the country took up most of his time and he could not devote as much attention to her as he would have liked. The only time they had together was usually at breakfast.

"Papa, I want another doll; one which can really talk," Marina would pounce on her father the moment he sat down to have breakfast.

"Yes, dear, your mama will take you to town tomorrow to buy you one."

"Is that so, mama? Will you take me to town tomorrow? I also need another dress, and a pair of shoes!" Marina would say with excitement.

"Of course, *Mwamikazi*, I will buy you everything you need," her mother would answer.

Marina loved pink dresses with white lace and frills at the hem. Her mother said that she looked like a little angel in them. She had also been taught how to dress appropriately for different occasions by her governess. And above all, she was taught how to carry herself like a lady. Whenever there was a wedding, Marina was chosen as the bridesmaid and she enjoyed the role enormously.

***

"Mabuja, you are worrying again. That is why you cannot conceive." Chantal was worried about her mistress. She was always frowning.

"Yes, Chantal, I am worried about my husband and my little girl. What will happen to us all ?"

"It's no use worrying *Mabuja,* we only have to pray. God will protect us."

"But the things I hear on radio, Chantal, I am so frightened!"

"Please don't be," Chantal assured her gently. *"Mabuja,* it's high time you gave your husband another baby, a boy this time. Marina is a big girl of seven now," Chantal would steer away the conversation to ease her mistress' tension. But the topic of conceiving was always unwelcome to her mistress.

Mukundane hated that talk; couldn't everyone see that she too needed another baby, not for her husband's sake but for her own?

"Yes, Chantal, I will give my husband another baby if God wishes," Mukundane replied curtly.

Marina was another constant reminder to her mother that she had failed to conceive.

"Mama, please, I want a little sister. Everyone at school has one."

"I know, *Mwamikazi,* just be patient; you will have a little sister or brother soon."

"I want a little sister, mama, not a brother. I will plait her hair and she will play with my dolls."

"Just pray, *Mwamikazi,* you only have to pray," her mother would assure her.

"And I will sleep with her in the same bed. And I will-"

"Marina, stop it!" her mother would cry in anguish.

9

***

Meanwhile, all groups opposed to the government had formed a consensus and the Rwanda Patriotic Front (RPF) was born. It was largely composed of the Tutsi who had fled their homeland in the 1959 putsch. It was rumoured that the RPF was planning to attack Rwanda and kill all the Hutu in the government.

***

When Marina was nine years old, her mother became pregnant again. It was the happiest moment in their lives. Marina jumped around the compound, overwhelmed with excitement. Chantal was overjoyed to have another baby to pamper.

Marina sewed tiny booties, dresses and hats for the coming baby.

"Aren't they adorable!" her mother cried when she saw the tiny garments.

Mukundane gave birth to a baby girl in February. The baby was the tiniest creature Marina had ever seen. Everything about her was small. But she was very beautiful with long curly hair. Marina named her Petite.

Petite was a difficult baby. She cried often and refused to suck her mother's breast. Chantal had designed her a big luxurious nursery but she could not sleep there and spent the whole night crying. Marina slept with her in her bed. She fed her with a bottle whenever she woke up at night and later sang to her. Petite would then drift off to sleep. Marina loved her very much, she was the little sister she had always prayed for.

***

On October 1st 1990, the Rwanda Patriotic Army (RPA), the armed wing of RPF, invaded Rwanda through the northern border with Uganda. The invasion was headed by Fred Rwigyema, who had been a senior officer in the Ugandan army, The National Resistance Army[NRA] of Yoweri Museveni. Museveni had four years earlier captured power after a five-year guerrilla war. There were also some senior Hutu officers in the RPA's top ranks like Colonel Kanyarangwe, who had once been a minister in the Habyarimana government. Pasteur Bizimungu was also a Hutu in the RPA's top ranks.

On the second day of their attack, the RPA suffered one of its greatest setbacks. Its leader, Colonel Fred Rwigyema was shot and killed. The enthusiasm for the war waned. The command went into disarray. Two days later, two other prominent Tutsi soldiers, Peter Baingana and Bunyenyezi were killed. Kigali, the capital of Rwanda, went into celebrations over the death of these soldiers, anticipating that with the death of its leader, the RPA's morale to fight would slacken.

Paul Kagame, another Tutsi soldier who had been away studying, came back and took over the command of the RPA. The conventional war was abandoned in favour of guerrilla warfare.

The Rwandese government, with the help of Zaire, Belgium and France, countered the attack. Tutsi and moderate Hutu who were suspected to be sympathisers of the RPA were rounded up, detained and tortured, among them, Bizimana. He was implicated in the newly formed opposition party and was perceived to be having greater links with the Tutsi. He was, however, released after the intervention of the international community.

As the war dragged on, incidents of isolated murders of RPA sympathisers were reported. *Kangura,* an extremist Hutu newsletter had published the ten commandments of the Bahutu. It read in part: 'Any Muhutu who befriends or marries a Mututsi woman shall be considered a traitor.'

The military commission had also issued a communique defining the 'enemy' of the government as 'any Tutsi, in or outside the country'. And the partisans of the enemy as any persons giving aid or support to the enemy.

Suddenly, Bizimana found himself 'an enemy of the government'. He was married to a Tutsi woman. As a measure of protection, he obtained a Hutu identity card for his wife (as many Tutsi were doing).

There were rumours that a group of young people known as *Interahamwe* (people who attack together) were being recruited widely across the country and trained as killers. As the *Interahamwe* were being transported by the truck load to their training places, they could be heard chanting the slogan 'we will exterminate them'. Them, meaning the enemy. The national radio began broadcasting propaganda, instigating the Hutu to kill the 'enemy'

'Hutu' inscribed on the walls of these houses. Death threats were being issued. Stones would be thrown on the roofs of these earmarked houses at night and doors banged with clubs.

***

One year later, Mukundane gave birth to the long awaited baby boy and he was named Pierre. He was a healthy lively baby who cried only when he was hungry. Everyone in the family doted on him.

Bizimana had started receiving death threats from the extremist Hutu in government who were convinced that he was supplying guns to the *Inyenzi* RPF and he was forced to resign his ministerial post. He contemplated fleeing the country but his wife, with a new born baby, made it impossible. Besides, he knew that he was being watched, every move he made being noted. His house too had been marked as one whose occupants were considered *abanzi* of the government.

Bizimana felt a deep sense of hopelessness. There was not much he could do to save himself and his family except to pray that those brutes in government would come to their senses and leave him alone.

Chapter Three

One night, Bizimana woke to the sound of gunshots. Fear gripped him. He had stood up courageously against the death threats ever since his house had been marked a week ago. Slowly, he got out of bed and tiptoed to the front door. He checked the bolts, they were all in place. But would that save him and his family, he wondered to himself. He tiptoed to the children's bedroom, where they were sleeping peacefully, their little faces as serene as those of angels. Petite, as usual was cuddled in Marina's bed, one arm flung carelessly across her chest. Pierre slept in the adjoining bedroom, his thumb stuck in his mouth. But the other side of the bed, where Chantal normally slept, was empty.

He wondered briefly where she was at that time of the night.

"Chantal?" he called softly. There was no answer. Maybe she was in the toilet, Bizimana concluded. He felt hot tears sting his eyes as he looked down at his children. God, he did not want to lose them, he prayed silently. He moved back to their bedroom. His wife, too, slept on peacefully. She stirred slightly in bed, but did not open her eyes. Bizimana opened the curtain, careful not to make any noise, and peeped through the window. The first rays of sunlight were beginning to appear on the horizon.

As if on impulse, his wife opened her eyes. He smiled down at her, not wanting her to see how frightened he was. He sat down on the bedside and took her warm hands in his.

"What is it?" she inquired sleepily. As if in answer to her question, there were more gunshots, this time closer. Mukundane sat up abruptly, startled. The sound of a heavier gun, something like a sub-machine gun, rattled in the air, close to their gate. Mukundane swiftly got out of bed and began struggling into a night gown.

Bizimana felt his legs go weak. He was frightened beyond words. He peeped through the window again but saw nothing.

"The guards! Where are our guards?" Mukundane whispered to her husband.

"They are of no use now. They are either collaborators, or they have been overpowered," Bizimana answered.

"The kids! Oh my God, my children, I have to get them!" Mukundane's voice was full of fear but her husband signalled to her to wait. More gunfire rapidly went off, causing tiny sparks to appear in the orange morning sky. When it finally died down, they could hear muffled voices at the gate.

"*Abanzi* of this government, bring forth yourselves before we set this house on fire!" a voice, full of authority, barked.

Mukundane halted at the sound of the bellowing voice of the soldier.

"Quick," Bizimana said. "Get the children and Chantal and hide in the ceiling."

"I give you three minutes before I set this house on fire!" the voice bellowed again.They could hear them forcing their entry into the house. With feigned machismo, Bizimana walked to the front door. There were about ten armed men in his sitting room. One of them, who looked like their leader, was sitting comfortably in the arm chair. He looked painfully at home. There was something vaguely familiar about him. The other soldiers were stationed at the two doors which led outside, carefully blocking the exits.Two soldiers covered Bizimana as he entered the sitting room. He found himself staring at the glistening barrels of their guns and their stone-cold eyes.

"Put your hands on your head and sit down," one of the soldiers ordered him.

Bizimana hesitated for a moment. He knew that defying the order meant death. Just for a fleeting second, he thought of escaping, but he did not see how he would get past the soldiers at the door without risking a fusillade of bullets to his head. Reluctantly, he did as he was told.

Their leader stood up slowly and came to stand in front of Bizimana. "Where are those guns?" he asked in a dangerously quiet voice. Bizimana stared at the soldier. Now that he had spoken he recognised him as the notorious no-nonsense Colonel Renzaho well known for his mercilessness. So the government had sent that bastard to finish him off, Bizimana thought angrily. He felt a cold shiver, born of both the early morning chill and the fear running through his whole body. Colonel Renzaho had used the invasion crisis to enrich himself by acquiring the businesses of the Tutsi who had fled the country after they were implicated in the invasion. He killed anyone who tried to get in his way.

"Those guns, *Nyakubahwa,* where are they?" the Colonel asked again as he stood towering over Bizimana.

"I have no guns, Colonel. You know that as much as I do," Bizimana answered in an annoyed tone.

"Oh yes, you have. them Those same guns you supply to the RPF, where do you hide them?" The Colonel's voice was thick with sarcasm.

"I have never supplied any guns to the RPF."

There was a sharp report of a slap. Bizimana's hand flew protectively to his cheek. The Colonel turned to one of the soldiers and gestured him over. The soldier came and pulled Bizimana by the collar and punched him hard in the stomach. Bizimana grunted and doubled over. The soldier pulled him up again and this time hit him squarely on the bridge of the nose. Bizimana felt his head spin and his vision blur. He gingerly touched the spot where he had been hit. There was blood oozing from his nose.

The soldier hit him again on the head with the butt of his gun. Bizimana cried out in pain. He felt himself blacking out, and as he struggled to retain his footing, he tripped and fell to the floor with a thud. He felt more than saw the Colonel's face close to his own, asking him again where he had hidden the guns. He tried to answer but there were bubbles of blood in his mouth.

"Search the house," the Colonel ordered the other soldiers. Six of the soldiers proceeded to the inner rooms to search for the guns.

***

Mukundane and the children were hiding under the beds in the children's room. Chantal was still nowhere to be seen. When the soldier opened the door to the children's bedroom, Mukundane froze in fear and stopped herself from breathing. The soldier stood in the doorway briefly, his eyes sweeping over the bedroom. Then without bothering to look under the beds, he closed the door and left.

After a while, the six soldiers assembled in the sitting room and informed the Colonel that they had not found any guns. By then, Bizimana had regained consciousness and was sitting up, his back against the wall.

"What about that *Inyenzikazi* wife of his and those brats, didn't you find them as well?" the Colonel asked.

The soldiers were quiet for a moment.

"Go and get them!" the Colonel barked at one of the soldiers. It was one of the easiest tasks the soldier had ever been asked to accomplish. Pierre was whimpering loudly, wanting to come out from under their confining hiding place. Petite was demanding her milk in not so quiet a voice. The noise led the soldier to their hiding place and he ordered them to come out.

"Please, no, leave us alone. We have not harmed anybody," Mukundane protested hysterically.

"Shut up, you *mvunamuheto!* Today you will die with your children," the soldier hissed. He caught Mukundane by the shoulder and dragged her to the sitting room, Petite and Pierre following closely.

"Where is my hus..." Mukundane began to say as they entered the sitting room but the words died on her lips. Bizimana's face was a mass of swollen tissue and broken skin. A dark smudge of blood had coagulated around his nose. His eyes were red and his mouth swollen.

"Oh...my...poor...man," Mukundane said between sobs. The Colonel was watching her in amusement. The gown which she wore had a long slit in front. A lump of shiny black pubic hair was visible as was a smooth thigh. An amused glitter appeared in the Colonel's eyes.

"Sergeant," the Colonel called one of the soldiers, "maybe we can use another method to make the *Nyakubahwa* tell us where he keeps the guns." The Colonel pointed to Mukundane. The Sergeant immediately understood.

"Very well, Colonel," he answered.

With the help of another soldier, they got hold of Mukundane and proceeded to pin her down on the floor. Mukundane kicked and squirmed, lashing out at the soldiers. The soldiers were momentarily shocked by her strength. One of them slapped her hard on the face. Mukundane let out a high-pitched wail.

Marina, who had been hiding in a different place, had also come out when she heard her mother's screams. She was now standing by the door leading to the sitting room, which was ajar, her body shaking with fear. She stood rooted to the spot, peeping through the door. There were about four soldiers in the sitting room who seemed to be on guard. Her father was huddled in the corner, his face unrecognisable.

Pierre was perched on the arm of the chair, his thumb stuck in his mouth. He was crying soundlessly. Petite was standing in front of one of the soldiers, her big frightened eyes looking up at him as if she wanted an answer to what they were going to do to them.

Marina felt a strong urge to go and comfort the two children, her fears momentarily forgotten. But just then her eyes caught her mother's figure. She was spread-eagled on the floor with two soldiers holding her down. A giant of a soldier was towering over her, consciously rubbing his manhood which was slowly forming a bulge in his trousers. He wore a stupid victorious grin and kept on licking his lips.

Marina felt a horrible nausea sweep over her. She wanted to rush to her mother and save her but her legs were cold and felt like logs of wood. She could not move them. As she watched, the Colonel struggled out of his trousers and stood there naked, his manhood obscenely pointing in front of him. In one swift movement, he was on top of Mukundane. She put up a feeble resistance but she might as well have reserved her energy. The two soldiers holding her down were too strong for her.

Marina closed her eyes. She willed herself to move but her legs let her down. She opened her mouth to scream but no sound came out. She heard the fabric of her mothers night gown ripping and her eyes involuntarily flew open.

She watched as the Colonel, with a vicious thrust of his body, entered her mother. Nausea rose to her throat like bile and she knew she was going to throw up any minute. Mukundane tried to push the Colonel away but only succeeded in igniting him the more. Like a possessed man, he began pounding at her. He slowed down briefly and looked in Bizimana's direction.

"Once you tell us where those guns are, I will stop doing this to your wife," he said breathlessly. But Bizimana's eyes were swollen-shut against the horrible scene in front of him.

With renewed energy, the Colonel resumed the pounding. Mukundane curled her fingers into claws and lashed out at him. Marina heard him curse under his breath but he did not slow down. Mukundane screamed out as the Colonel seemed to tear at her insides. Marina too let out an anguished cry but it was muffled by her mother's. She managed to drag her cold and shivering body through the corridor, then to the kitchen and stopped only when she reached the backyard. She fell down as vomiting spasms racked her body.

17

Bizimana too seemed to be galvanised into life by his wife's scream. He opened his swollen eyes and stared at her, spread-eagled on the floor and the over-weight Colonel on top of her. He felt a surge of blinding rage involuntarily overwhelm him. He tried to stand up but his head was throbbing dangerously and he knew he would never manage to reach his wife in time to save her. He groped around blindly for an object which he could use to hit the Colonel.

His eyes landed on the Colonel's gun, which he had thrown in the chair in a hurry. But he dropped the idea as soon as it had crossed his mind. He had never fired a gun before. Besides, he could not muster enough energy to lift the gun and hit the Colonel with its butt. He groped again and this time his hand came up with the baton the Colonel had been carrying. In his haste, he had thrown it under one of the chairs. His hand closed on the baton, and very slowly, he began to crawl to where his wife lay.

Pierre had stopped crying and was watching the scene before him, mesmerised. His eyes landed on his father. He made a noise indicating he had seen his father and even pointed at him.

"Shut up!" his father mouthed. Pierre seemed to understand the gravity of the situation and did not attempt to say anything.

Bizimana looked at the Colonel on top of his wife. The Colonel's eyes were closed tight and he seemed on the verge of an orgasm. His wife was gritting her teeth in pain. Like a shark would circle its prey, he resumed crawling towards his wife. But Pierre's noise had attracted the attention of one of the soldiers stationed at the door. He glanced at Bizimana and saw the baton in his hand. He must have guessed what Bizimana intended to do.

"Don't even think about it," he warned. But Bizimana's eyes were fixed on his wife. The two soldiers holding her down had relaxed their hold and were staring intently at the movement of the Colonel's body; their eyes shining with desire as they awaited their turn.

With lightning speed which even surprised himself, Bizimana lunged savagely at the Colonel, and with the baton in one hand, he hit him on the head with all the energy he could muster.

For just a fleeting second, there was no reaction. The Colonel was jerking away involuntarily when the pain seemed to penetrate, and he withdrew abruptly. Jets of semen splashed the two soldiers near him and they backed away. With the soldiers out of the way Bizimana raised the baton and before the soldier who had given the warning could stop him, he hit the Colonel once more on the head.

All hell seemed to break loose then. The two soldiers near him snapped back to attention. The others keeping guard at the doors came in in a mad rush. The Colonel was writhing in pain, clutching his head which was bleeding profusely. Mukundane lay on one side, whimpering in pain and shame, desperately trying to cover her naked body.

Bizimana saw a blur of movement as the soldier who had issued the warning drew his gun and pointed it at him. Before he could take cover, he was sprayed with bullets from all angles. The walls of the sitting room were splashed with blood and tiny pieces of flesh. The Colonel, too, did not stand a chance of survival against the two heavy blows he had received from the frenzied Bizimana. A few minutes later he died.

Chapter Four

There was chaos in the sitting room. The soldiers were shocked by the Colonel's death. Mukundane was like a person in a trance. She was unsure of her surroundings. Her first instinct was that she was dead. What with all the gunshots. When she realised that she could move her hands, she was more confused.

Petite and Pierre were crying hysterically. They called out to their mama, papa, Chantal or Marina to come and rescue them but nobody took any notice of them. Petite, overwhelmed by the sudden change of events, rushed to her father's body and began shaking him.

"Papa, please wake up," she said to the bullet riddled body of her father.

One soldier was talking to Mukundane. She could only see the movement of his lips, but could not hear a word.

"Madam, now we have to depend on you to tell us where those guns are. Your husband has stupidly got himself killed. And," the soldier paused, "we were told to use any, or all the methods to obtain the information."

Mukundane stared blankly at the soldier. There were humming sounds in her ears. Without knowing it, she had begun to cry.

"Okay," the soldier who had taken over command said, annoyed. He beckoned to another soldier and pointed to Petite. The soldier caught hold of Petite and brought her forward. She began to whimper and tried to break out of the soldier's grip. The soldier looked down at her and smiled thinly. "Don't worry, honey, no harm will come to you if your mama tells us where those guns are hidden." He drew his bayonet.

Petite, on seeing the shining weapon, sensed danger. She let out a deafening scream and broke away from the soldier's grip. She ran to the door and collided with Marina, who had been awakened from her stupor by the loud gunshots.

Marina too, was in a state of shock and confusion as she dashed from one room to another screaming for somebody to come and save them. She held Petite protectively in her arms. The soldier who had followed Petite to the door grabbed her and pulled her from Marina's arms.

"No, please, don't harm her, you can kill me instead!" Marina begged, breaking into fresh sobs.

"Don't worry sweetie, your turn will soon come," the soldier answered. The soldier, who now had Petite in a firm grip, brought her to stand in front of her mother. She was trying to fight off the soldier with her frail arms. "Any answers?" the soldier asked Mukundane.

"Let my little girl alone, I know of no guns," Mukundane sobbed, her senses coming back to her. The soldier did not bother to press for an answer. He pierced Petite through the stomach leaving the bayonet stuck in her. Petite let out a choking wail, then fell back with a screech of pain.

Marina felt herself screaming, but actually no sound was coming out of her dry throat as she watched the horror scene in front of her. Mukundane put her head between her knees, wanting to block out the scene in front of her eyes. The soldier who had bayoneted Petite now had Pierre by the shoulders. He pushed the frightened, shivering boy in front of his mother.

"Those guns, madam, surely now you can tell us!" But this time, Mukundane was oblivious to her surroundings. The events of the early morning had taken their toll. She collapsed and was enveloped in darkness. She felt herself falling into a deep bottomless pit.

"Okay," said the soldier who had taken over command. He handed his bayonet to the one holding Pierre. He stuck it in Pierre's neck and the little boy collapsed on the floor. Marina screamed and this time there was sound from her dry throat. But it came out as a high- pitched wail. The soldiers glanced in her direction but ignored her.

"Waste her too," the soldier who had taken over command ordered, pointing to Mukundane. A bullet was put through her head and she died instantly.

Marina jumped at the sound of a gun going off so near her. With dazed eyes, she looked around the sitting room; at the horror scene, and felt the same nausea rise up in her throat, like it had when her mother was being raped. Her only thought then was to put as much distance as she could between herself and the slaughter house which had once been her home.

21

Without warning she broke into a run, past the soldiers, who had now relaxed their guard. She had no recollection of how she managed to run through the gate. She heard the soldiers cock their guns and braced herself for the coming bullets. The fear inside her spurred her on and she ran like she had never run before.

One soldier also took off after her, but their new commander called him back.

"Don't waste your energy, she is only a child and she won't get far," he said.

The soldiers stood for a few minutes staring at the bodies in front of them.

"They did not have any guns, did they?" one of them commented.

"What if they didn't?" their new commander shot back angrily. He glanced back at the bullet riddled bodies and the slaughtered children. For the first time, he seemed to notice the dead Colonel.

"My God! How are we going to explain the Colonel's death?" he exclaimed. "Let's get out of here!" he shouted.

"But...Sergeant..." one soldier began to say.

"Move it!" their new commander snapped. "We have another family to take care of," he said matter-of-factly.

***

Marina passed many familiar houses but dared not stop to ask for assistance. She continued running until she realised she was in a different neighbourhood, then stopped. She looked up and down the road; it was deserted. She stood there for a moment, not knowing what to do. Then she heard the sound of a heavy vehicle. She dived behind the shrubs by the roadside. The vehicle was an army truck and it carried a few soldiers. Marina held her breath as the truck passed by. The mere sight of soldiers left her throat dry and jolted her mind to the events that had occurred earlier that morning.

She lay behind the shrubs for a while, pondering what she would do next. She only wished to sleep and never wake up to the dreadful world. She felt physically tired and emotionally drained. She was hungry and thirsty. She relaxed her muscles and lay back.

"Oh dear God, what am I going to do?" she sighed. She closed her eyes, not wanting to remember anything that had happened that morning. But a kaleidoscope of images kept on whirling in her mind, her mother spread-eagled on the floor...

22

She must have dozed off. When she opened her eyes, dusk was falling. She was disoriented and did not know where she was. She looked around her wildly. She was lying in the cold grass and her body felt stiff. Then the events of that morning came back to her.

I must run, was her first thought. Slowly, she got to her feet and peeped down the road; it was deserted again. Her second thought was to make a plan of how she was going to elude her enemies. She had an aunt, her father's cousin, who lived in one of the suburbs. She would go there and tell her what had happened. Then she would call in the police and they would arrest those soldiers who had murdered her family! But to reach her aunt's house, she had to go back to their house to get the correct bearings because she was not sure where she was now.

Which part of the city am I, she wondered.

She dreaded even just going near their house. She never wished to see that house again.

She began retracing her way to where she had run from. And, there, not far from where she had been hiding, stood their once beautiful home. In her small mind, she had imagined that she had run very far from that 'slaughter house', but actually, she had only gone round their house.

The sitting and dining rooms were in darkness but there was light in her parents bedroom. She skirted the house and came to stand at her parents' bedroom window. After looking more closely, she realised there was somebody moving in the bedroom. She looked more closely and heaved a sigh of relief when she realised who it was. Marina ran to the door and opened it. "Chantal!" she cried out.

Chantal stopped in her tracks and turned around.

"Oh Chantal! They...have..., they have..."Marina could not bring herself to say the words. She only wished to bury her head in Chantal's warm bosom as she had done many times before and feel comforted.

Chantal was staring at Marina coldly, her face twisted in anger.

"Chantal! Mama, Papa, and..." Marina tried to tell her again.

"Don't come near me, you *Inyenzi,*" Chantal snapped.

"Oh, Chantal, it is me, Marina, do I look so horrible?"

"I said stay away from me! I know who you are all right, with Tutsi blood flowing in you!" Chantal spat out.

Marina backed away, momentarily puzzled.

"Chantal, what are you talking about?" she asked in a frightened voice.

"What I'm talking about is that this country is fed up with the likes of you. And that we shall cleanse it of all *Inyenzi.*"

Marina stared at Chantal in utter disbelief, not knowing what to make of her speech. For the first time, she looked around the house. The closets in her parents' bedroom stood empty. There were about four suitcases lying on the bed, stuffed with mostly her mother's clothes.

The whole house looked bare and many boxes stood in the corridor, presumably full of property which belonged to them. Marina jumped at the sight of two soldiers who sat in the kitchen. One was smoking a cigarette and the other was drinking canned beer.

"Chantal I...don't...understand.." Marina stammered.

"No you don't, little one," Chantal answered with a stiff smile. "Your parents," Chantal continued in a quiet whisper, "were *abanzi* of this country. They deserved to die. So do you." Marina flinched at the venom in Chantal's voice. She was too shocked to even think of what to say.

"I...thought...you...were my mother's friend." Marina said with tears glittering in her eyes.

"Me? Your mother's friend?" Chantal laughed dryly. "Never, my dear."

"And...my father...once saved your life," Marina was crying loudly.

"Your father?" Chantal shouted. "He was a murderer! He just murdered my husband, Renzaho, the only man I ever loved." There was sadness in Chantal's eyes. "Now I wish I had not left this house at night when he told me to. I could have saved him." She continued in the same sad tone. "And your father saved me, you say? Not really. He had wanted me to rot in prison. He was a heartless son of a bitch. I hated him. I hated all of you."

"You...mean...all these...years...you...only pretended!" Marina said, petrified. "You ought to feel guilty."

Chantal smiled complacently. "I was later paid by the state to spy on your parents," she said.

"And now you are stealing our property too!" Marina burst out. She had stopped crying. She was now more annoyed than afraid of Chantal. "And," Marina continued, "I don't believe those lies that you were being paid. Your are only a...a..." she struggled with the right word to describe Chantal, "a treacherous woman!"

"Don't you stand there and talk to me like that, you *Inyenzi*," Chantal said menacingly. "You don't seem to understand what your fate is, do you?" she sneered. "Your race is now a banished one. "And," she added, "we shall save you from the humiliation of dying by a matchet." She turned around and gestured to one of the soldiers. Marina snapped to attention. She seemed to realise what the soldier was about to do to her. On the spur of the moment, she shot through the door. Chantal and the two soldiers were taken unawares and did not react for a few seconds.

"Quick, she mustn't be allowed to escape this time," Chantal shouted at the two soldiers. Marina had managed to go as far as the corner which curved into a neighbour's compound and by the roadside stood an old vehicle. The bonnet was open and it did not have an engine. Without thinking, Marina jumped right inside and closed the bonnet.

"She can't be far from here," Chantal kept on saying as the search for Marina intensified. At one point, one soldier came close to the old vehicle. Marina was frightened to death, but the soldier glanced casually at the old vehicle and did not bother to search inside.

The neighbour's houses were searched but Marina could not be found. After about three hours, the search was abandoned.

"We shall seal off all the exits," the soldiers suggested. "By morning we shall have found her."

Marina listened to all this from her hiding place. She would rather die of starvation than risk the cruel death at Chantal's hands, she decided. A truck was parked at their gate and boxes, suitcases and more boxes were loaded on it. The truck kept on coming back and each time it left fully loaded. It seemed its destination was not far because it made about four trips as Marina watched from an opening in the old vehicle.

Marina wondered where Chantal would be taking their property. Then she remembered something Chantal had said, that the notorious Colonel Renzaho was her husband! Could it be true or was Chantal simply...

With shocked horror, Marina remembered how she had once found the Colonel in their kitchen talking quietly with Chantal. The driver had picked her up from school before the time for breaking off because she was not feeling well. Chantal had been caught off-guard and it had showed visibly on her face.

"Ah... Marina, go to your room, I will bring you the cake I have been baking for you." She had smiled at her. From her bedroom window, Marina had watched the Colonel drive away in his sleek Mercedes soon afterwards. She was sure he was the man she often saw on television and remembered her father saying how cruel he was.

She remembered mentioning it to her father and how uncomfortable it had made him feel. He had promised to ask Chantal about it.

The notorious Colonel had been coming to their house and Chantal was his mistress! Together they had planned her family's killings. A terrible fear flowed down her spine. She also remembered that Colonel Renzaho's house was not very far from theirs because she had heard the driver who picked her from school talk about it, and even point at the posh big house. She could not imagine how Chantal had managed to deceive them all when behind their backs she was planning their murder.

By daybreak, Marina had not left her hiding place. She spent the whole day under the hot confining bonnet. But by evening, she could not stand it any more. When dusk began falling, she struggled out of the old vehicle. Her whole body felt cramped and her legs were stiff. She felt pain in the limbs as she took her first steps in almost two days. But she was determined to escape, nothing would stop her this time.

She began to walk.

At first she walked in circles, not sure of where she was going. She had abandoned the idea of going to her aunt's place. She was not sure if she hadn't turned into an enemy as Chantal had. Besides, it would be the first place where the soldiers would look for her. She had now established a pattern; she was walking north of the city of Kigali. Her only wish was to leave the town which had brought her so much suffering and pain. She aimed for an exit to take her away from Rwanda forever. Like Chantal had said, her race, her mother's race to be precise, was now banished from Rwanda.

***

It was a slow wearing journey. She had to dive into bushes every time she heard a car approaching. Gunshots seemed to be erupting from everywhere. During the night, she slept in ditches and when day broke, she struggled to put as much distance as she could between her former home and her destination. She rejected any offers of rides on bicycles and in cars, but ate the little food which strangers gave her, whenever she stopped somewhere to rest. Her legs were swollen and her eyes bloodshot from crying. Her hair was unkempt, her dress torn and dirty.

When she eventually stumbled into a camp at the border town of Katuna some days later, she was on the verge of death.

There were some other displaced people in the camp, most of them children. There was a white priest who welcomed her. She was given food and water but she was too sick to eat anything.

The white priest informed Marina that he was from Uganda. He told

26

her that when she got better he would take her with him.

Away from Rwanda, Marina thought happily.

But one week later, Marina's health had not improved. She deteriorated with each passing day. The white priest got concerned. What did those brutes do to the poor girl, he thought angrily. He tried to talk to her.

"What is your name?" he asked her.

"Don't know," Marina answered.

"Where is the rest of your family?"

"Petite? I don't know where she is! Someone snatched her from me! Where is she?" Marina shouted.

"Who is Petite?" the white priest asked calmly.

"Yes, yes, now I remember, even Papa and Mama! Where are they?"

There was a glassy look in her eyes. The girl was not only very sick but also deranged. "What horrors has the poor girl been subjected to?" Father Marcel wondered.

Chapter Five

Father Marcel arrived in the small township of Hoima, Western Uganda, in early 1959 at the age of thirty. His assignment was to head a newly formed parish situated 43 kilometres south-east of Hoima town.

The small parish, as Father Marcel later found out, was almost non-existent. The few believers around prayed under a tree with a catechist presiding over Mass. Father Marcel slept in the single tiny grass-thatched house which had been built by the Christians.

His immediate task was to build a church. He worked closely with the catechist, who mobilised other believers. They made the bricks locally and got timber from a nearby forest.

Next, Father Marcel constructed his own small brick house which he shared with the catechist and his family. He then turned his attention to enlarging the number of believers. Almost the whole community, where the parish was situated, was entrenched in their cultural beliefs and did not know much about God and his kingdom.

He persuaded young boys and girls of school-going age to come to the parish and learn the catechism. He often visited the elderly and strengthened their belief in God. He also visited young couples and urged them to get properly married in church and have their children baptised.

His big motorcycle roared like a hungry lion, raising a lot of dust as he plied the narrow village paths on his pastoral work.

The local people had learnt to identify its sound from far and would hide whenever they heard him coming. They were tired of his gospel of 'One God' while they themselves had many gods whom they wor-shipped and offered sacrifices to.

Only the children welcomed him. The young boys held him in awe and longed to touch his white cassock and feel his soft golden hair. They were amazed by the long rosary with large beads which fell to his knees.

But what amazed them even more was the big motorcycle and the noise it made as it spurted to life after he had kicked it several times. The younger ones would run away thinking that it was going to eat them. But he would call them back and make them sit on the large motorcycle. They would giggle and beg him to give them a ride.

"If you come for Mass on Sunday, I will take you for a ride," he would assure them.

"Will you also give us sweets?" they would ask.

"Yes, even shirts and shorts."

"What about shoes?"

"Yes, even shoes, but only those who come for Mass on Sunday."

"Father, for me I want those ones like Matayo's," one boy said. Father Marcel turned and looked at Matayo. The boy was about six years old, but ever since he had come to the parish to learn the catechism, he had refused to go back home. He moved with the Father wherever he went.

"Yes," he answered at length, "you will get shoes like Matayo's." And true to his word, he would offer the children many presents and the following Sunday, many more would go for Mass.

Some courageous young couples did go to the parish to be properly married. They were regarded as courageous because of the grilling interrogation Father Marcel subjected them to before they received the sacrament of Holy Matrimony.

He would inquire, in minute detail, about the background of their brides-to-be. In the years he had spent at the parish, he had come to learn that African marriages survived on the credibility of the woman more than the man. It was, therefore, vital to marry the 'right' woman in order for a marriage to stand the test of time.

"Mukazi murungi?" (Is she a good woman?) Father Marcel would start his interrogation, speaking in his usual heavily accented Runyoro.

"Ego, Taata," (Yes, Father) the groom-to-be would answer solemnly.

"Tabungabunga?" (Is she faithful?)

"Ego, Taata."

"Amanya Ruhanga?" (Is she religious?)

"Ego, Taata."

"Iwe toina bisuzi?" (Don't you yourself have bastards?)

This question always made the young boys uneasy. They had tried to explain to the Father that according to African culture, there were no children called bastards. Children were children in the eyes of their parents. But Father Marcel was adamant. He maintained that all children born outside wedlock were *bisuzi*. So the young boys had learnt to answer in the negative whenever he posed the question, otherwise he would not marry them.

Slowly, the number of believers increased but not to the level Father Marcel would have wanted. The people were still sceptical about the religion which preached the doctrine of 'One God' and required them to shun their other gods.

One day, several years after Father Marcel had built the church, he came back from his pastoral work to find Matayo, his young assistant, as the people now referred to him, down with a high fever. He was also vomiting and having convulsions. Father Marcel administered some drugs to him. The next morning the temperature had subsided and the vomiting stopped. But violent spasms were still racking his body.

Father Marcel, worried about Matayo's worsening condition, called the catechist and other people at the parish to join him in prayer for the sick boy. By midday, however, Matayo's condition had deteriorated and he was gasping for breath. Everyone knew that he would not see the light of the next day.

Father Marcel hastily summoned Matayo's father who came promptly. He took one look at his sick son and declared that he needed to treat the boy at home.

Father Marcel was astounded. "But what is the use of taking him deeper in the village where there is no medicine? I would rather we took him to the referral hospital in Hoima town," he tried to reason with Matayo's father. Matayo was slowly drifting into a semi-coma.

"He doesn't need any hospital, Father," Matayo's father answered calmly.

"But look at his condition!" Father Marcel insisted. "He needs the hospital alright."

"No, Father, he doesn't. I know quite well what is wrong with him," Matayo's father insisted.

Father Marcel gave in. He regretted why he had called the sick boy's father; he could have rushed him to hospital instead. With the help of other young men, they strapped Matayo on the bicycle like they would a dead body, covered him with a blanket and took him home.

On arrival, Matayo's father immediately took the sick boy to the family's ancestral shrine. It was a huge tree trunk with a small hut built in front of it. Father Marcel watched in utter consternation as Matayo's father slaughtered a white goat, then a cock and poured the blood on the tree trunk. He called upon the gods of the sun, earth and the god of mercy to heal his little boy. He then ordered Matayo's mother to remove all her clothes and sit in front of the shrine holding Matayo, as he continued to offer more sacrifices of food and invoke the mercy of the gods.

After that, the sick boy was carried inside the house and forced to drink some bitter herbal medicine. A fire was lit in the middle of the hut and more herbs thrown in it. They produced thick smelly smoke which was fanned into Matayo's nostrils. The sick boy immediately sprang to life and began coughing and sneezing. Father Marcel left soon after that. Matayo, it seemed was now out of danger.

When he went back to check on Matayo the following day, Father Marcel was astonished to find him playing with his brothers, completely cured!

"You see, Father," Matayo's proud father said, "even our gods do heal and protect us, just like your mighty God does."

Father Marcel was stunned into silence. He could not believe that it was the same Matayo who had been unconscious only the previous day! What kind of powers do these so-called gods have, he wondered to himself.

"Matayo," Father Marcel said, "how are you feeling now?"

"Quite fine, Father. I would like to go back with you now," Matayo announced.

"You are going nowhere with that white-skinned so-called priest!" Matayo's father burst out.

"But I learn many good things at the parish," Matayo pleaded, surprised by his father's outburst.

"You learn nothing at the parish, your place is here at home where you will learn the ways of our people," his father said, his eyes dancing with fury.

"Please, Father Marcel, tell him what you teach us at the parish," Matayo begged, on the brink of tears.

Father Marcel, who had listened to the exchange between father and son, was silent for a moment. He could not understand Matayo's father's venom and hatred for the parish. At the same time, he could not argue with Matayo's father now because the latter was very angry. He would try to talk to the irate father after his anger had subsided.

"You have to listen to your father, Matayo," Father Marcel said quietly. "You cannot disobey him, but I promise I will be coming to visit

31

you," he said with a gentle pat on Matayo's shoulder.

"But, Father, I want to go back with you now. I want to learn the catechism," Matayo was now crying. Father Marcel smiled at him apologetically and began moving towards his motorcycle. He kicked it twice and it spurted into life.

"I hope this is the last we see of you," Matayo's father shouted after him.

Farther Marcel smiled stiffly and rode away amidst Matayo's wails of protest. His mind was preoccupied as he rode to the parish. He was sorry that he had lost one of the most keen students he had. But what else could he have done. It was not easy to be accepted by these people, he had to gain their confidence slowly.

Two days later, however, he was surprised to see Matayo walk into his office.

"What happened Matayo?" he asked standing up to embrace the young boy. "Did your father finally allow you to come?"

"I ran away," Matayo stated with a mischievous smile.

"Matayo, I thought I warned you against rebelling against your father!" Father Marcel said, trying to sound tough. But deep inside, he was glad that the boy had come back. "Suppose he comes for you and forces you to go back home?" he asked him after an interval.

"He won't," Matayo answered quickly. "He hates the parish so much." He laughed. "Besides, I won't agree to go back with him."

Father Marcel was silent. He knew from experience that African fathers attached a lot of value to their sons. Matayo's father was bound to come for him and take him back by force, unless...

He looked again at the young boy in front of him. His face was serious and determined.

He is a rebel, Father Marcel thought to himself. Just like I was.

A thin smile appeared on his lips, spreading to the corners of his mouth as he remembered how he had defied his own father. He could not prevent the memories which came back to him in a rush, plunging him back in time when he was fifteen years old.

Chapter Six

Marcel's father, Orsin, too had hated the Catholic church with a passion. He had hated it for having allied with Austria to suppress their nationalistic struggle for independence during the unification of Italy.

Orsin, like many young boys of Naples of his age, belonged to the 'Red Shirts' army, which had been formed by Garibaldi, a veteran soldier, to fight for the political freedom of the people of Italy from the oppressive Austrian domination.

Long after the unification of Italy had been attained, however, Orsin's hatred for the church did not go away.

He never permitted any of his children to be baptised, let alone attend church service. But his eldest son, then known as Angelo, was a rebel from childhood. He often defied his father and attended church service.

Angelo tried to reason with his father that his hatred for the church was obsolete. The church laws, with their special law courts and sanctuary powers, which Orsin had hated most, had been abolished. But Orsin was a man who never budged. When he found out that Angelo was defying him, he ordered him to stop attending church service or find himself another home. Angelo chose the latter and at the age of fifteen, he ran away from home and joined the Catholic priests of Sicily. He was baptised and his new name became Marcel.

He was taught the ways of God and later became an altar boy. A few years later, he was ordained a deacon which prepared him for the priesthood. But he would never be ordained a priest unless he obtained the blessing and permission of his parents which he knew he would never obtain.

But Marcel's passion for the priesthood could not be ignored. It was

33

decided that he be sent to Africa as a missionary. Marcel arrived in Uganda at the age of twenty five and was first placed in the good hands of the Verona Fathers of Mbuya, who determined to model him into a good priest. Five years later, he was sent to Hoima to start a parish of his own.

As he looked at young Matayo in front of him now, he too remembered the rebellious spirit which had possessed him when he was still young.

"Matayo, how many sons does your father have?" he asked the small boy.

"Many, five, maybe, ten, I'm not really sure. Why do you ask?" Matayo asked the Father slightly confused.

"Never mind," Father Marcel answered with a smile. "You are welcome to stay at the parish for as long as you wish, Matayo," he told the young rebel. Matayo smiled shyly and moved out of the office.

The Matayo incident however was an eye opener. Father Marcel realised that there was need to construct a small dispensary which would pass for a hospital for the local community and where the local people could be treated. This way, they would not resort to their gods for healing.

With renewed vigour, Father Marcel set out to construct the dispensary. It was a slow process because there was not enough labour as the people were not sure what implications a 'hospital' would have for their community. They were, therefore, reluctant to offer their labour.

The funds were also not easily available and Father Marcel had to write to his superiors in Italy for assistance. A year later the dispensary was completed. It consisted of two rooms, one a ward for the seriously ill and the other for dispensing drugs. A trained nurse was sent from the big hospital in Hoima town to man it. She treated minor ailments and referred the complicated cases to the main hospital in town. They never went there and instead went back home to die.

The nurse also doubled as a midwife. A few women, mostly first-time mothers, came to the hospital to deliver their babies. These were scorned by the elder women and referred to as 'cowards'.

"It's a waste of time," the elder women would say. "After all, we have experts in our villages who are even better than that so-called nurse."

About a year after the dispensary had been opened, a young girl of 16 years was brought to the hospital to deliver after the traditional birth attendants in the village had failed. She had been carrying twins;

the traditional birth attendants had succeeded in delivering one of them but the second one had failed to come out. The young girl was bleeding profusely and was in great pain. She had spent two days in labour. A few hours after she arrived at the hospital, she died, but miraculously the baby survived.

Her husband, who had all along insisted on taking her to a witch-doctor instead of the hospital, claiming that it was the evil spirits at work, went berserk. He threatened to chop the nurse into small pieces. He was only calmed down by Father Marcel, but in 'revenge' he walked away, leaving the baby behind.

Father Marcel knew another problem had cropped up. More irate fathers and relatives would abandon their babies at the dispensary or would simply not be in a position to take them. He had to provide a place where such children could be kept and that's when the idea of constructing an orphanage came to him.

The orphanage was constructed without much difficulty. It was only one long bare room. The children in the orphanage were those whose mothers died in childbirth at the dispensary. But as people came to know about it, children who were physically abused by their parents ran away from home and came to live at the orphanage. Even those whose parents had died a long time ago wanted to live at the orphanage.

The orphanage was placed under the care of Sister Bernadette, an elderly nun who was one of the 'founders', as Father Marcel referred to them, of the parish.

The orphans were moulded into religious people. Some of the girls were groomed to become nuns while some boys were trained for the priesthood.

They had to grow crops in order to raise enough food to eat. They sold some of what they grew to raise additional income to maintain themselves. They also grew fruits and baked pancakes which they sold.

Matayo, the young 'rebel' had grown into a tall, handsome young man with big laughing eyes. He was a jolly person with a good sense of humour. He was adored by the people at the parish and was always ready to give a helping hand whenever the need arose. He felt pity for the unfortunate orphans, some of whom had lived at the orphanage since the first day of their lives and was the only home they knew, Sister Bernadette, the only mother they had.

Matayo would tell them stories to make them laugh and forget their miseries.

Everyone knew Matayo was slated for the priesthood. He had been at the parish longer than anyone else and had even received formal education. Besides, he was Father Marcel's favourite.

Father Marcel, however, had other plans for Matayo. He knew from experience that Matayo would never be ordained a priest without the permission and blessing from his parents. But Matayo could join the vocation of brotherhood since permission from one's parents was not a prerequisite for becoming a brother.

***

One hot afternoon, Father Marcel had gone to Matayo's small room which was just behind his own residence. He dreaded waking up the poor boy from his nap to send him to the village in the hot sun. But he was the only one who knew the new catechist's house and so there was no alternative.

Not bothering to knock, he pushed open the door and what he saw almost left him blind.

He gaped at the two black shining bodies of Matayo and a girl from the orphanage, on Matayo's bed, engaged in the act of fornication. Their bodies were drenched in sweat and they were heaving uncontrollably.

He stood there for a full minute before the two 'sinners' noticed his presence. When Matayo finally saw him, he jumped off the girl and hurriedly began pulling on his trousers, his face full of shame and shock. Father Marcel closed his eyes. He could not bring himself to look at the naked girl, nor did he want to see the betrayal in Matayo's eyes. Like a defeated man, he walked out of the room.

He did not see Matayo again until the following day and only because he had summoned him to his office. Father Marcel had waited for Matayo to go to him, repent and receive the sacrament of penance but the boy had chosen to avoid him. He was disappointed, to say the least.

When Matayo entered Father Marcel's office, he was still shaking with fear. His eyes were fixed on the ground and he looked as if he would be happy if the ground suddenly opened up and swallowed him.

"My son, what tempted you to do such a sinful act?" Father Marcel began. Ever since Matayo had come to live with him at the parish, Father Marcel felt he shared some sort of kindred spirit with the young boy. In the fifteen or so years they had been living together, a special attachment had grown between them.

"The devil, Father," Matayo answered, tears welling up in his eyes.

"Haven't I taught you to be ready for the devil's long arm and told you that he can reach anywhere and present himself in any form?" Father Marcel asked, his voice rising in anger.

"Yes, Father," Matayo answered in a small voice.

"Then what happened, my son?" Father Marcel shot back, his voice laced with impatience.

"It was a mistake, Father. It will never happen again," Matayo replied.

"Very well, my son, it is good you accept that you made a mistake. Come for the sacrament of penance tomorrow."

"Thank you, Father," Matayo answered before he fled the office.

Father Marcel sat alone in the office for some time. He then called in Sister Bernadette and told her what had happened.

"We have to remove that girl from the orphanage," Sister Bernadette said, outraged. "She will spoil all the other girls."

"I know, Sister," Father Marcel said in support of Sister Bernadette's decision. "She can't stay here anymore; she will tempt Matayo again by her presence."

"I will send her to the orphanage at the big parish in Hoima," Sister Bernadette said as she stood up to leave the office.

"Thank you, Sister," Father Marcel said with a smile. "But...er...er..." Father Marcel hesitated before he continued, "nobody else should know about this...this..." he groped for the correct word to use. "This...er er ...you know," he ended vaguely. Sister Bernadette nodded in understanding.

"You should not mention it to anyone," Father Marcel continued, as if he was not convinced by Sister Bernadette's mere nod of the head. "Ah... you see...after Matayo has expressed his desire to join the brotherhood, this incident would be unfortunate if... people got to know about it."

"Of course I won't," Sister Bernadette said, a tinge of annoyance creeping in her voice.

"I am sorry, Sister," Father Marcel said, embarrassed by his overzealous protection of Matayo. "Of course I trust you, Sister," he continued, laughing self-consciously. Sister Bernadette stood there briefly before she left the office, her face contorted in anger.

Father Marcel felt sorry for her. He should never have pushed her that far. How could he not trust her with a secret. After all, she too had a past to conceal.

He remembered the first time he had met her. She was in hospital because she had attempted to commit suicide. He had talked her out of it and brought her back with him to the small parish and he had convinced her to take up the vocation. Since then, she had never looked back and she was one of the most committed nuns Father Marcel knew.

Sister Bernadette kept her promise and the girl was sent to the orphanage in Hoima with a small note from Father Marcel saying she should be watched closely.

As he reflected on his success and failures in those years, he could not fail to blow his own trumpet. He had built the small parish from scratch. Within years, it had grown into a big sub-parish then to a complete fully fledged major parish, with him as its head.

The dispensary had also become a fully fledged hospital manned by two doctors and several nurses. The convent, which Sister Bernadette had helped start, had fifteen nuns in it. There was a farm too, which had been started as a project for the orphans and now was the biggest in the area, with cattle, pigs and chickens.

At sixty years, Father Marcel had almost forgotten that he had never been properly ordained as a priest. But who cared now.

What hadn't he done for these people of Africa? His mentors back home in Sicily would be proud of him.

Chapter Seven

Sister Bernadette had recently received more orphans than the orphanage could accommodate. Father Marcel had brought them from his trip to the war-torn Rwanda. Their parents, as Sister Bernadette learnt, had been brutally killed and Father Marcel had found the children huddled in camps, trenches and ditches.

"This is a better home for them," Father Marcel had informed her. "At least here we can provide them with shelter and food."

And so Sister Bernadette had struggled to improvise beddings for the new orphans. Sometimes three people slept on one mattress. The children were malnourished, and some were on the point of death. They were severely traumatised and constantly had nightmares. They called for their mothers and screamed if anyone tried to hug them, thinking it was an enemy. The older ones said they never wanted to see their homes again, the young ones said they wanted to go back home.

Father Marcel had said the children had been exposed to the most horrid and bone-chilling experiences which had left them permanently traumatised.

"Apart from shelter and food, they will also need our understanding and care," Father Marcel had told the community at the parish.

Sister Bernadette had set herself to nurse them. She encouraged them to talk about the horrors they had gone through because it would help ease the pain.

Most of them were eager to open up, but in the middle of the narration, they would break into uncontrollable sobs. Sister Bernadette was always there to offer a shoulder to cry on. Who could blame them. The world had dealt them a heavy blow.

Slowly, the children were beginning to show some signs of life and adapt to the new environment. The younger ones had picked up the local language and spoke it almost fluently.

But the healing process was not going well for one young girl in particular. She was always secluded and had completely refused to open up to anyone. Not even the ever-smiling and jolly face of Matayo moved her, nor the easy-going nature of Father Marcel.

She kept everything bottled up in her heart. Her eyes were always sad and empty as if they had seen very many bad things. Her smile, which was as rare as a blossoming flower in the dry season, never reached her eyes. It was a mere parting of the lips. Sister Bernadette placed her between eleven and twelve years.

"Father, one of the girls you brought is completely impossible; she does not talk to anyone and she is a bit strange," Sister Bernadette had complained to Father Marcel about the girl.

"Who is this, Sister?" Father Marcel inquired.

"Marina."

"Ah...that quiet girl. She will come through, just give her a little more time," Father Marcel assured the Sister.

"But Father, she is not only quiet, she is really strange," Sister Bernadette insisted.

"You see, when I found Marina, she was...was...disturbed," Father Marcel could not bring himself to say the word deranged.

"All right, Father, let's try to work a little harder with her, maybe..." Sister Bernadette shrugged helplessly.

"Please do that," Father Marcel smiled convincingly at Sister Bernadette.

But Sister Bernadette knew it was not going to be an easy task. Marina had something about her which Sister Bernadette had failed to figure out, but she was certainly different from the others. Was it the lady-like way she carried herself, like a princess despite the awkward circumstances at the orphanage? Or the self-sufficiency kind-of-air she always exuded? Marina looked like she did not need anyone in this world.

Despite all that, the girl was a smashing beauty. Her legs were long and shapely, her waist tiny and one could easily tell that her bum was going to be rounded and soft. Her hair was black and curly, but she neglected it and did not bother to comb it. Her big round eyes were beautiful though they did not smile.

Like most orphans who had come from Rwanda, Marina feared hard labour. She had confided in Sister Bernadette that she had never held a hoe in her life. Sister Bernadette had started them off with light work like sweeping the dormitory and fetching water, but still Marina could not perform any of those small chores.

The dormitory was one long room partitioned into two. One half was occupied by girls while the boys slept in the other half. The floor was made of mud and as a result, it usually became dusty, a perfect breeding place for jiggers.

The bed-wetters were allocated the extreme ends of the dormitory and they shared mattresses, but still each morning, the stench of urine filled the whole dormitory.

Sister Bernadette was the most feared nun. She was especially strict with the girls, and every evening, after the orphans had eaten their supper and said their evening prayers, she would call those aged between eleven and sixteen years to talk to them. The topics ranged from sex education to how a proper lady should behave. The girls were normally shy and never asked any questions.

If she sent any of the girls on an errand, she would spit on the ground and tell the girl that she had to come back before the spittle dried up. Of course by the time the girl came back, it would have dried up and the girl would be put to task to explain why she had delayed.

Sister Bernadette also taught the girls about personal hygiene. She never allowed them to share dresses, because some of the older girls had ringworm and other skin infections. She told the girls that if they shared belts, they would contract menstrual pains from those who suffered from that ailment during their periods. But the girls knew how to prevent that. If any wished to share a belt, two girls would hold the belt on either side, and the one who intended to put it on would jump over it. That way, she would not contract the 'disease.'

***

Marina still kept away from all these 'girlish' intimacies. And so, when after a year after her arrival at the orphanage something very shocking and terrible happened to her one morning, she had no one to turn to; no one to confide in. She woke up to find her dress marked with blood drops. When she attempted to walk, more blood oozed from her private parts and trickled down her thighs. It was warm and dark red.

Marina screamed out aloud and some girls came running to see what had happened to her.

"Marina, what is it?" a girl called Stella Maris who had become Marina's friend asked in a concerned voice.

"Blood," Marina cried out. "It's all over me! I don't know what could have happened to me."

Stella Maris looked at the other girls and they exchanged knowing looks. "Here, let me see;" she said. "Where is the blood coming from?"

"Down here," Marina said touching her buttocks.

"You must go and see Sister Bernadette immediately. She will tell you what to do," Stella Maris told Marina.

But I have done nothing wrong...and...Marina began to say, but the girls urged her to go and see Sister Bernadette all the same.

When she told Sister Bernadette about the blood coming from her private parts, she took her to an inner office and told her to lie on the table and open her legs wide. Sister Bernadette placed two of her fingers inside Marina's vagina and probed gently.

"It's okay Marina," she said with a smile, "you have now become a woman just like I keep on explaining to you during those evening talks."

"But Sister, you never tell us where the blood comes from?" Marina pointed out.

"Where else did you think the blood would come from?" Sister Bernadette snapped, evidently annoyed, "through your nose?"

Marina kept quiet. She feared the Sister so much that she dared not annoy her.

"Well," Sister Bernadette said, relenting, "I will show you what to do." She got out a roll of cloth, commonly known as 'Jinja' and cut off about a metre. The material was normally used to make uniforms for the orphans who attended school.

Sister Bernadette cut the metre into small pieces which she folded neatly. She placed one piece under Marina's private parts and told her to keep the rest and change the cloth whenever she bathed. Marina was warned not to throw the first pieces of cloth away because Sister Bernadette would need them.

When Marina took the first piece of cloth Sister Bernadette had inserted in her, she was surprised when she was told to hand it over to an older girl who was seated on a chair.

"But Sister, it is all soaked in blood and it...it...smells awful," Marina said, shocked.

"I know that, Marina. Here, give it to me."

Marina unwrapped the piece of cloth from a polythene bag and gave it to Sister Bernadette.

"Remove your blouse," Sister Bernadette told the girl seated on the chair.

The girl did as she was told. Sister Bernadette began rubbing the blood-soaked cloth on the girl's back, then under her breasts. Some of the blood trickled onto her stomach. Sister Bernadette explained that the girl had ringworm and the used pad was the only medicine which could cure her.

The following day, Marina was called to Sister Bernadette's office to see how she was getting on.

"I am fine, Sister," Marina answered shyly.

"Did you wash your private parts with soap and warm water as I told you?"

"Yes, Sister."

"Good," Sister Bernadette answered, satisfied. "Now, I want you to rub this egg in your armpits every time you bathe. It is the first egg to be laid by one of our hens and it will protect you from growing hairs in your armpits," Sister Bernadette explained.

Marina felt like laughing but did not dare. She did not know whether to believe Sister Bernadette or not.

" Sister," she said uncertainly, "for how long should I use the egg? I mean the medicine."

"Just a week, Marina, and you will be saved from those smelly hairs."

Next, Marina was given a leaf from one of the climbing plants known as *orwihura*. When squeezed, the leaf produced a sticky, dark green juice. Marina was to use the juice to wash her private parts every evening. It was to protect her hymen and keep it intact until she was ready to be married.

The whole of that week, Marina was subjected to eating and drinking various bitter herbs. These were to produce more fluids in her body which would be released when she had sex.

Marina found all these frightening. Sometimes she felt like crying and refusing to do as she was told, but then very few people disobeyed Sister Bernadette.

"I will have to take you to the famous *muko* tree," Stella Maris told Marina after she was through with the various herbs she had been given to drink.

"What for?" Marina inquired warily. She hoped it was not to eat more bitter herbs.

"Come on," Stella Maris said, "you will soon find out." Stella Maris had a piece of broken clay pot with her. When they reached the tree, she pulled down one branch and told Marina to pluck off some leaves and squeeze juice out of them and it into the bowl-like pot. Then she ordered her to squat and drink the juice.

After Marina had finished, Stella Maris released the branch.

"What was that all about?" Marina asked puzzled.

"That juice will protect you from getting menstrual pains," Stella Maris explained.

With all the rituals completed, Marina was initiated into the club of women. At thirteen, she was no longer considered a girl. And with that, and perhaps the strong relationship which was growing between her and Stella Maris, Marina seemed to have shed some of her inhibitions.

Chapter Eight

Marina was slowly turning into a star. She was always in the limelight at every occasion which took place at the parish. She was called upon to serve tea whenever there were visitors at the orphanage or at Father Marcel's house. When the Bishop visited and said Mass in their small church, Marina would take both readings for that Sunday.

Each month, one girl from the orphanage was assigned the duty of arranging the altar. All the girls liked the job because it meant less work. They were rotated monthly so that each girl got a chance to work at the altar.

But Marina had been working at the altar close to three months now. The other girls were grumbling quietly, accusing Sister Bernadette, who normally drew up the roster, of favouritism. But if only the girls knew, they would be accusing Father Marcel who had insisted that Marina be left to work at the altar permanently.

"She is meticulous, tidy and very clean," Father Marcel would defend his decision. "She does the work better than all the others."

Every Saturday evening, Marina would collect fresh flowers for decorating the altar in preparation for Mass the next day. She would put them in two big vases and place one vase at either side of the altar. She would also place some flowers on the statues of the Holy Virgin Mary and her child Jesus, and that of Saint Joseph, the worker. She would also cover the various boxes which were placed around the church with spotless white pieces of cloth, being careful not to cover the inscriptions on them which read thus: 'Gifts to Saint Jude of the hopeless cases', or 'Pray for the souls in purgatory' or 'Gifts to Saint Maria Theresa'. Christians dropped money in these boxes through tiny openings which had been left at the top of the boxes. Marina often wondered who removed that money. Or did it go directly to the saints it was addressed to?

Lastly, she would place candles on all the statues and on the altar, ready to be lit in the morning when Mass began.

Marina enjoyed her work enormously. It gave her the peace and quiet she always missed while in the noisy dormitory. She would muse over the power of God as she worked at the altar. She felt closest to him then and did not dare utter a single word.

Work at the altar also meant that she wouldn't have to go to dig, a task she dreaded most. She hated having to soil her legs in the mud because her feet would develop cracks and her back would ache for hours after the digging in the morning. Those who went to dig in the morning brought back food for lunch and had to pass by the well to wash and bring water to prepare lunch.

Those who had remained behind sweeping the dormitory and compound would cook the lunch. Lunch was normally served as late as 3 p.m. and then the children were allowed to rest up to 5 p.m., after which they would start preparing supper. Supper was eaten as early as seven o'clock to enable the children to say their evening prayers and recite the rosary, and the girls to attend Sister Bernadette's evening talks.

By the time they went to bed at about ten o'clock, Marina would be completely worn out, only to be awakened at 5 a.m. to begin another hectic day, which started with digging.

But work at the altar was light. Marina only had to wash the table cloths once a week, mop the floor and dust the pews every once in a while.

One Saturday, as she was preparing to leave the church after cleaning the altar, Matayo peeped in to greet her. He grinned at her in the fatherly manner he always used for the girls at the orphanage and Marina returned the smile shyly.

"Good work, Marina," Matayo observed, pointing at the fresh roses on the altar table.

"Yes," Marina answered.

"My, aren't they lovely?" he continued, flashing her one of his warmest smiles.

"I guess so," Marina answered without much interest.

"Are they fresh?" Matayo asked again. He seemed undeterred by Marina's dismissive response.

"Yes," Marina replied curtly. She was getting irritated. Matayo was a very jolly person with a wonderful sense of humour. He treated the girls at the orphanage like his daughters. He was always there to help in case one required his assistance. But Marina hated to make small talk and most of the time, she did not know what to say. The new language she had had to learn was still a problem and she could not express herself well. Besides, she did not want to say much in case she divulged anything about her past which she wished to keep hidden.

She now hastily cleared the petals of flowers which had fallen on the floor, picked up the bucket and made ready to move out.

"Here, let me help you with these," Matayo said, taking the broom and bucket from her. Marina did not have the heart to refuse; she only wanted to get away from Matayo's ever smiling face.

Outside the church, it was turning chilly. The sun was just setting but at this time of year, the place was always cold in the evenings and hot during the day.

Marina looked up to see Father Marcel strolling towards his residence. He saw them too and raised his hand in greeting. Matayo beckoned him to stop and he walked towards where the Father stood.

"I say, Father, how is the evening? Coming from a walk?" Matayo said to the Father in form of greeting.

"Yes, my son," Father Marcel replied. "It's a bit chilly though."

"Yes, Father, but with that cassock, you should be warm enough," Matayo smiled at the Father.

"Age, my son, it's age. It chills your bones, you know," Father Marcel answered with a sigh.

"You mean age has finally caught up with you?" Matayo teased the Father good-naturedly. Father Marcel had refused to slow down despite advice from the doctor to take it easy.

"Sixty one years is not particularly young, my son," Father Marcel said with a rueful smile.

Marina caught up with them and knelt down to greet the Father.

"Yes, my daughter, how are you today?" Father Marcel returned Marina's greeting as he patted her on the shoulder.

"I am fine, Father," Marina replied.

"Good."

"So, Father," Matayo interjected, "I want to get your advice about this stubborn new-born calf. It has refused to suckle and it grows weaker every day."

"Oh yes, that stubborn calf, what shall we do with it?" Father Marcel asked worriedly.

"I don't know, Father, and if we don't do something, it will soon die." Matayo's otherwise beaming face was now filled with worry. He extended the same kindness he showed people to animals.

Father Marcel turned to Marina.

"Any ideas, young girl?"

"We...I don't know," Marina said hesitantly. "We could feed it with milk using a bottle..."she ended uncertainly.

Father Marcel smiled at her sweetly. "You think so?" he asked. "But as you know, our Matayo here is a very busy man; he has to look after all those other calves, isn't that so, Matayo?" Father Marcel asked now turning to Matayo.

"Yes, Father," Matayo replied regretfully. "I wouldn't possibly find enough time to feed that one calf."

"I...could do it, Father," Marina chipped in, her face beaming with excitement. "I know how to feed babies." Her eyes were shining and her face as radiant as the early morning sun.

"You do?" Father Marcel asked in astonishment. Matayo too was staring at Marina, his eyes full of surprise. He had never seen Marina so excited.

"I could try," Marina said, backing down a bit and annoyed at herself for having displayed such lavish emotion. Suppose they asked her which babies she had fed.

"All right," Father Marcel said, "I will talk to Sister Bernadette tomorrow and see if it won't interfere with your work schedule at the orphanage."

"Thank you, Father," Marina said happily. Deep inside, she really wanted to feed that calf and save it. If she hadn't managed to save her little sister, then at least she could save the calf. She had to pinch herself hard to stop this train of thought. She had sworn never to think about her dead family.

"All right then, I will see you both tomorrow," Father Marcel said by way of bidding them farewell.

Matayo picked up the bucket and broom which he had put down while talking to the Father. "I will see Marina to the dormitory," he said.

"Good night, Father," Marina bade farewell to Father Marcel.

Father Marcel replied, "Good night Marina." He took a few steps and then he looked back at the receding figures of Marina and Matayo.

It's good she is picking up, he thought to himself. She has come a long way, but who can blame her. Only someone who never saw her the day she walked into the camp back in Rwanda. Father Marcel sighed and continued to his residence. His back ached and his legs felt weak. His teeth were chattering uncontrollably. He pulled the collar of the cassock more tightly around his chin. Maybe the doctor was right. He had to slow down and get more rest.

Age, he thought bitterly. As Matayo had said, it had finally caught up with him.

***

The following morning, when Marina went to the farm, Matayo was already there. Marina had been excited when Sister Bernadette had informed her that she was free to go and feed the calf.

"Where is the stubborn calf?" she asked Matayo after they had exchanged greetings.

"In here," Matayo replied, opening the wooden shelter where the calves were usually kept to stop them from sucking all the milk from their mother's udders before Matayo could milk them.

Marina pulled the calf from the shelter and stroked its head gently. The hairs at its nape were as soft as cotton wool. It reminded her of her dead sister, Petite. She put the milk, which Matayo had squeezed from its mother's udder, in a feeding bottle. It was still warm and foamy. Sister Bernadette had provided her with the bottle, one of the old ones she had once used to feed the babies at the orphanage.

She bent down and began feeding the calf. Matayo watched in fascination. She handled the calf so expertly, as one would a baby. This girl is an enigma, Matayo thought to himself. She never ceased to surprise him; she took naturally to everything she did in her quiet way. The calf drank all the milk.

"Thank you," Matayo said quietly. "You just saved its life."

Marina did not reply. Images were whirling in her mind. She was lost in another world as she remembered vividly how she used to feed Petite. Tears stung her eyes, but she forced them back. She had sworn never to cry again; she must be strong and forget the past. The calf was staring at her as if it wanted to say that it was grateful. She stroked its head again and it mooed gratefully. The sound the calf made sounded so much like Petite's whenever she was sated after a good meal. The tears she had been holding back flowed freely down her cheeks.

Matayo was watching her strangely. He had never seen Marina cry before. "What is it, Marina?" he asked softly, moving to her side.

Marina did not answer; she tried to control the tears without much success. All the memories of that ghastly day back in Rwanda came back with such a vengeance, forcing her body to shake violently. The tears she had successfully locked up in her head seemed to come loose as if in rebellion. Matayo put his hands on her shoulders in a comforting gesture.

"Come on, Marina, you know you can tell me anything," Matayo coaxed her gently. He pulled her by the arm slowly until she was standing on her feet. Then turned her around to face him.

In an instant, Marina was in Matayo's strong and comforting arms, her body racked with sobs. Matayo held her tightly. He did not know what else he could do to comfort her. Marina felt surprisingly comfortable in Matayo's arms and did not want to leave them. It reminded her of how she used to bury her head in her mother's bosom whenever she felt unhappy. She now felt she could trust Matayo to take away the unhappiness she felt, just like her mother used to do.

After a time, she disengaged herself from Matayo's arms and stood dabbing at her eyes with the corners of the sleeves of her blouse. "I am sorry," she said after an interval.

"Sorry for what?" Matayo asked softly. "Look, Marina, you don't need to be embarrassed for showing your emotions. Cry if you want to or laugh, nobody will arrest you for that. And," Matayo continued in the same soft tone as if he was talking to a child, "you can always confide in me, tell me anything, Marina. It will do you a lot of good. Like what made you cry just now?" Matayo asked.

Marina stared at the ground but did not say anything.

"Remembered something?" Matayo probed gently.

Marina nodded, more tears welling up in her eyes.

"What was it, Marina?" Matayo was now pleading with her. He did not want to frighten her off after he had calmed her down.

"I...I..." Marina tried to speak but the tears were choking her.

"Come on," Matayo led her by the arm to the hedge near the wooden shelter and made her sit on a stump of a tree. He too perched himself near her. "Tell me everything," he said quietly.

Marina blew her nose, not knowing where and how to start. It had been a year now since she had been at the orphanage; such a long time! Yet in a way, it seemed just like yesterday when she had stood in their sitting room in Rwanda staring at her family lying dead.

"My parents, brother and sister were all killed," she began. At first, they were inane disjointed words that just spilled from her lips, but after a few sentences, she gained confidence and spoke more firmly. She told Matayo everything she could remember and he did not once interrupt her. When she had finished, she felt like a heavy load had been lifted from her shoulders.

"And you say you walked from your home in Kigali to this camp?" Matayo inquired.

"Yes," Marina answered.

"How many days did you spend on the way?"

"Not days, it must have been weeks. I can't be certain."

"And there you met Father Marcel?"

"Yes, but at that time, I only knew him as the white priest from Uganda."

"How many days did you spend at the camp?"

"A week maybe, I'm not so sure again."

Matayo was silent. He remembered Father Marcel mentioning that he had to spend three weeks at the camp waiting for Marina to recuperate.

"Why are you asking me all this?" Marina asked, her voice laced with fear.

"No, it's nothing," Matayo answered soothingly.

He was annoyed with himself for having probed too deep. And he did not even know why he had done it. Maybe it was that disturbing knowledge at the back of his mind which Father Marcel had confided in him about Marina being deranged when he had found her. But it did not matter now. He could understand what the poor girl had gone through.

"I guess I have to be going back. Sister Bernadette will wonder what could have happened to me," Marina said, bending down to pick up the feeding bottle.

"All right, Marina, I will see you again tomorrow," Matayo replied.

In the days that followed, Marina continued to go to the farm to feed the calf. It had become some sort of ritual and she knew she would miss the calf when it eventually got stronger and was weaned.

A sort of special attachment had also grown between her and Matayo. He always managed to make her laugh and she trusted him. He had also become one of her friends at the parish, including Stella Maris.

In the one and a half years Marina had been at the orphanage, she had blossomed into a young beautiful woman of fourteen. With the encouragement of Stella Maris, Marina now cared more about her body and even plaited her hair.

"We are now young women," Stella Maris would say. "Very soon, we shall be married."

"Married!" Marina echoed. "At fourteen!"

"Yes, Marina, some girls at the orphanage get married at that age."

"Not me, Stella Maris," Marina said, annoyed that her friend could even suggest such a thing. "Besides, I want to ask Father Marcel if he could allow me to attend school like the other young orphans."

Stella Maris shrugged. "Wish you luck then," she said.

When Marina approached Father Marcel about her intentions to study, he was not very encouraging. "It is a good idea, Marina, but...is it really what you want to do?"

"Yes, Father, I want to continue with my studies," Marina said excitedly.

"Let me think about it, Marina, I will let you know after Christmas," Father Marcel said and added, "that would mean sending you to the Hoima orphanage, because here we only teach the young ones."

"It's all right, Father, I would still come back here for my holidays," Marina said confidently.

Father Marcel smiled at her; he did not relish the idea of sending her away to strangers. It might take her a long time to get used to them.

Chapter Nine

The Christmas season was normally a big event at the parish. The orphans, nuns, priests and the medical personnel at the small hospital all came together to celebrate the birth of Jesus Christ.

The elderly widowed women who lived at the parish, and others who had never been married, and the catechists and their families, all joined in this merry-making event. Some of the believers who were too poor to buy meat for the big day also came to the parish for the traditional Christmas feast.

It had always been Father Marcel's policy to slaughter a bull for Christmas. He would also distribute gifts to the community at the parish, his priority being the orphans. He always assigned a nun the duty of wrapping gifts such as dresses, sweaters, shoes, shirts and trousers in small boxes.

These boxes would be arranged on a large table on the eve of Christmas and separated according to the age and sex of the intended recipients. The orphans would each be called upon to pick a box. This way, no one would complain of being side-lined or accuse Father Marcel of practising favouritism.

But Father Marcel always sought out Marina to inquire if what she had picked fitted her well and if she liked it. If she raised any complaint, Father Marcel would offer her more gifts. Nobody knew of their little secret, not even Sister Bernadette. But Father Marcel had an answer to defend his act in case anyone came to learn of it. "Marina always takes the readings on Christmas and so she has to look extra smart," he would say.

Only one Mass was celebrated on Christmas Day and it did not begin until midday. Father Marcel wanted to give ample time to everyone to cook their meals and dress carefully in their new outfits and then come to church fully prepared to celebrate Christ's birth. The nuns built the 'Nativity scene' where Jesus was born, and decorated the whole church.

Father Marcel's sermon for Christmas emphasised the third mystery of Nativity of the rosary. He urged the believers to be tolerant even in poverty.

"The son of God himself chose to be born in a cow-shed when he could have been born in the best hospital in the world," his voice would echo in the church as the believers listened attentively, not wanting to miss a single word of the important message.

Marina, having dressed in her smart new dress and shiny shoes, would feel elated as she took the second reading: "You will become pregnant and give birth to a son, and you will name him Jesus. He will be great and will be called the son of the most high..." her voice would ring out solemnly. She would then end by saying, "Brethren, stand up and acclaim the holy gospel."

After Mass, everyone went into the shed, which had been built in front of the Father's residence, to eat and drink and make merry. Father Marcel would pass around, greeting everybody and wishing them a merry Christmas. He would then distribute bottles of altar wine and the faithful would 'indulge' in a little drinking.

Matayo was usually one of the happiest people each Christmas day. He played the piano to entertain the merry-makers. He would then present his small choir which he recruited from the altar boys and other school boys. During the Christmas season, Matayo, with his small choir, visited the faithful to sing them Christmas carols and in return collect small gifts of food and money which would help prepare the big day. This house-to-house visit to the faithful went on for about a week.

After presenting his choir, Matayo would drink about two bottles of wine and then take to the floor. Only church music would be played, but Matayo somehow always found a way of dancing to its rhythm, sending many roaring with laughter.

That year's Christmas, however, Matayo was 'peaceful,' as Father Marcel said of him when he was not jumping up and down in the name of dancing. He was sitting with the guests, sipping from a bottle of altar wine.

Marina too was having a good time. She was seated next to Stella Maris and they were back-biting people.

"Marina, I wish we could have some wine too," Stella Maris said.

"How can you say that, Stella! You know we are not allowed to take any form of alcohol."

"I wouldn't call altar wine alcohol, now, would you, Marina?" Stella Maris challenged her friend. "There," she pointed to where Matayo was seated, "let's go and ask him for some wine."

They moved to where Matayo was seated and joined him.

"Hey, girls, enjoying yourselves? Remember, this is Christmas Day," Matayo said, his face breaking into a wide grin.

"We would if only we could take some wine like you are doing," Stella Maris answered.

"Here," Matayo said offering his bottle to Stella Maris. "You can drink some."

Stella Maris took a few sips. "Yah, it tastes good," she said.

"Take all of it if you want," Matayo said generously. "I will get another bottle from Father Marcel; and Marina? Is she not taking some?"

"I don't know," Marina answered uncertainly, "I don't think we are allowed to do so."

"Oh come on, Marina," Matayo said persuasively, "today is Christmas and we are all supposed to enjoy ourselves."

"Look at it this way," Stella Maris said, turning to her friend, "if you say this is alcohol, why does Father Marcel offer it to us during Holy Communion? And why did Jesus himself change water into wine at Cana and offer it to the guests at the wedding party?"

Marina did not have any answers; she gave in and took a sip of the wine. It tasted delicious and she took some more.

After a time, Matayo's wife joined them. She was a young girl, not much older than Stella and Marina. She had been with them at the orphanage. When Matayo had announced his intention of marrying her, the community at the parish had been surprised. They had all thought that Matayo was slated for 'bigger' things. But Father Marcel had blessed their marriage, so...

The two girls had been her bridesmaids and since then, they had become friends.

"How's the baby?" they asked her in unison.

"He is fine," she answered with a smile. "He grows bigger every day and resembles his father so much," she ended with a glance at her husband. Matayo went and brought another bottle of wine and the four settled down to enjoy the drink.

"This has been a quiet Christmas," Matayo observed. "I wonder if there's a football match this evening."

"I doubt it," Stella Maris answered. "It wasn't announced in church and besides, it's already getting late." The sun was setting, casting its last rays over the horizon.

"I enjoyed last year's match; we beat those boys from Hoima parish, remember?" Matayo said.

"Oh, I remember that vividly," Stella Maris answered with a light shining in her eyes. "I was the chief cheer leader and after the match, Father Marcel prepared another feast for us."

"Let me go and check on the baby," Matayo's wife announced. "He must be awake by now, demanding for his meal."

"I will go with you and take a stroll. I'm already bored, just sitting here," Stella Maris said. The two young girls left and Marina remained behind with Matayo.

"Won't you have some more wine?" Matayo asked her.

"No, thank you. I guess I have taken more than enough. I can feel my head throbbing."

They sat in silence for some time. Matayo had learnt never to push Marina when she said 'no'. He treated her like a gem. It had taken him a long time to gain her confidence and trust and he did not want to spoil it. He was also glad that Marina had eventually got another friend. At least she was no longer living like a hermit.

Dusk had begun to fall when Marina stood up to leave.

"I will see you to the dormitory," Matayo told her.

"No, thank you, Matayo, I can manage alone," Marina answered.

"It's no bother, really. I want to make sure that you are not eaten by hyenas on the way," Matayo said.

Marina smiled warily. "All right," she agreed reluctantly. She took a few steps and staggered.

Matayo put out his hand to steady her. "Here, let me hold your hand," Matayo said. Marina surrendered. She had consumed much more wine than she could handle. They were halfway to the dormitory when she began feeling nauseous.

"Matayo, I want to vomit!" she cried out before she bent and vomited everything she had eaten for lunch. After a time, she stopped. There were tears in her eyes and Matayo gave her a handkerchief to wipe them away.

"Are you all right now?" he asked her worriedly.

Marina nodded her head.

"What you need is some fresh air," he told her gently.

He guided her to a tree and she sank down gratefully, sitting with her back against its trunk. "Careful," he warned. "There could be a python waiting to bite off a small piece of your behind."

Marina managed a weak smile. She wished she was in her bed in the dormitory. Her head was throbbing and she felt dizzy. Matayo noticed her discomfort and said, "Don't worry, just relax and the evening breeze will make you feel better." She took Matayo's advice and relaxed, leaning her head against the tree. After a time she felt better; the cold wind had blown in her face and the effect of the wine was wearing off.

Matayo sat down beside her. "Let me tell you a story about hyenas," he said. "It will make you happy. The hyena is the most greedy animal on earth, yet the biggest coward," he began. "If you smeared blood on a stone, he would swallow it thinking it was meat."

Marina laughed. "I have never heard that before; you must be making it up, Matayo."

"Honest!" Matayo said seriously. "It's quite true: you just don't know Mr Hyena. One day, he was hiding in the bushes waiting for Mr Luck to come his way. Then he heard a mother reprimand her child for wailing at night. 'If you don't keep quiet immediately, I will throw you to the hyena and he will eat you,' the mother said angrily.

"Hyena listened and knew he was likely to have a good meal that night. He waited by the window the whole night, but no child was thrown out to him."

"Oh poor hyena, why doesn't he go out and hunt for himself?" Marina asked.

"I told you he is a coward. Another time, he was hiding in the forest, as usual, waiting for his luck when he saw a man pass by. The man's arms were swinging to and fro as he walked, and poor hyena, in his small mind, thought that the arms were going to fall off anytime. He began salivating as he followed the man."

"Matayo!" Marina laughed. "Stop making up stories, and now, I really must go to the dormitory."

"It's good to hear you laugh," Matayo said. "Now I know you are all right. I will escort you to the dormitory."

All of a sudden, a dog barked close to where they were seated. Marina jumped and let out a frightened cry.

"Easy," Matayo said, pulling her down to her sitting position.

"I'm afraid of dogs," Marina said in a small voice.

"It's all right, Marina, that dog won't bite you. I know the sound of dogs that bark like that: they are toothless and as cowardly as an old woman."

Marina smiled in the dark, her fear forgotten.

Instead of sitting on the ground, Marina accidentally sat on Matayo's leg.

"Ouch!" Matayo let out a painful cry.

"I'm sorry," Marina said, "where did I hurt you?"

"Here," Matayo replied, guiding Marina's hand to the spot where he felt the pain. "My God, Marina, you are so strong I heard my bone crack!"

"Oh no, Matayo, you can't be serious."

"Here, feel for yourself, the bone is cracked!" Matayo said, now guiding Marina's hand to his shin. Marina rubbed the spot tenderly. Her fingers felt soft on Matayo's bare skin and had a soothing effect on him. He did not want her to stop.

He closed his eyes and something seemed to snap in his head. He felt his body go on fire and a blinding urge to make love to Marina took hold of him. The wine he had taken, coupled with the long day's excitement had taken their toll. He was like a person in a trance and some devil seemed to have entered him and was now responsible for his feelings. His manhood began to harden.

He grabbed Marina and clasped her to his chest, then pressed her body to his aroused manhood.

Marina was taken unawares. "Matayo, what is it?" she asked in a voice full of fright. Her first thought was that Matayo had seen a wild animal and was trying to protect her.

"Sh sh sh," Matayo hushed her up. "It's okay, Marina, I won't hurt you," he said in a husky voice.

"Hurt me?" Marina was now confused. She peeped at him through the faint light from the moon. His eyes were dazed and had a faraway look in them.

He is drunk! Marina thought to herself. I must run away from him. She tried to struggle out of his arms, but he was too strong for her. He pinned her to the ground, then with one arm, he began unzipping his trousers. In one swift movement, Matayo had removed the trousers and was trying to part Marina's thighs, using his legs. Marina then knew what Matayo intended to do to her.

"No, no," Marina began screaming and tried to put up a fight. But she was too feeble to ward him off. Images of her mother, spread-eagled on the floor and the Colonel on top of her, flashed through her mind. She also remembered the agony-filled sounds her mother had made.

Matayo was holding his elongated stiff manhood in one hand, while he used the other hand to keep Marina pinned to the ground. He began forcing himself inside her. Marina felt an excruciating pain tear through her body as Matayo entered her. He pumped at her and probed inside her with his enormous manhood. His torso was jerking up and down, establishing a consistent rhythm.

Marina began to whimper in a low tone. Matayo's mouth quickly closed over hers and he began kissing her, drawing the air out of her lungs. He thrust his manhood deeper inside her with renewed vigour. Marina cried out in pain and once again tried to push Matayo off her body but Matayo was making animal sounds and his eyes were closed. He gave one last, hard thrust inside her before he withdrew. His heavy body remained on top of Marina for a while and he continued heaving and breathing fast.

Marina lay there, all energy drained out of her. Eventually, when she managed to push Matayo's bulk off her, her first thought was that her private parts were torn out because she felt a lot of pain down there. She touched them gingerly, they were covered with a warm sticky liquid.

Matayo then seemed to wake up from his stupor and realise what he had just done. "Marina...Marina..."he said in a quivering voice. "Oh my God, what happened, what possessed me?" He pulled on his trousers and stood there gazing at her. "I...I...must escort you to the dormitory."

Marina just sat there, saying nothing, and continued to weep quietly.

Matayo placed his hand on her shoulders, urging her to stand up.

"No..." Marina screamed as loudly as she could and jumped as if Matayo's hand was full of thorns. "Don't...touch...me," she cried, backing away from him.

"Marina....please. Let me explain..." Matayo said uncertainly. But Marina kept on backing away, her eyes full of fear. When she had put enough distance between herself and Matayo, she broke into a run.

Matayo took a few steps to follow her, but when Marina realised it, she started screaming and he stopped in his tracks.

Marina entered the dormitory, breathless and crying hysterically. It was in darkness. She traced her way to her bed, and slumped on it.

"Marina, where have you been?" Stella Maris, who slept next to her asked.

Marina did not reply. She slid into the bed, pulled the blanket over her head and pretended to be asleep.

"Hey, Marina, how was your Christmas?" Stella Maris teased her.

But still Marina did not reply.

Chapter Ten

With Christmas over, life returned to normal at the orphanage. It was still a dry season and there was not much digging in the fields. It was harvest time. All the crops seemed to have ripened at once. Groundnuts were ripe but because the soil was so dry, it was difficult to uproot them. The children would struggle to pull them out of the dry soil, and often, had to use hoes to dig them out. It was a tiresome exercise and by evening the children's hands would be covered with blisters. They, however, enjoyed eating the raw groundnuts. They would munch them noisily and Sister Bernadette would reprimand them for their lack of manners.

"If you eat them raw, then I will not allow you to eat the cooked ones," she would shout at them. "The mixture will make your stomachs growl and you will pass bad air!" The children would only laugh but nothing would stop them from eating the delicious cooked groundnuts known as *nyamubugyo*.

Millet grains were ripe too. The children had to cut off the millet heads with very sharp knives. It was another tiring job and the children had to spend the whole day in the fields. The millet heads would be put in gunny sacks and carried back to the orphanage. Then they would spread the millet in the courtyard, which would have been smeared with cow dung a week earlier for that purpose.

Once the millet was dry, the children would thrash it using pestle-like sticks until the grains fell off. The grains would then be winnowed and stored in granaries.

Fruits like mangoes, guavas, strawberries and passion fruit would also be ripe at that time. The children's favourite were, however, mangoes.

They would wake up at 5 a.m., crawl through the barbed wire into the

Father's residence and pick the mangoes which would have fallen at night. Each child had a type that he/she preferred and whoever woke up first would pick the most delicious from particular mango trees. They would hide the mangoes under their beds and eat them at lunch time when they came back from the fields.

Running stomachs were the result of eating so many fruits at a go and sometimes the children would develop fever, but these were minor ailments which would go away without treatment.

Marina did not take part in the fun of the hectic dry season. Father Marcel had fulfilled his promise made earlier in the year and sent her to Hoima to attend school. Contrary to Father Marcel's initial fears, Marina did not find much difficulty in adapting to the new environment and making new friends. She had become more outgoing and friendly and was generally liked by the community in Hoima.

She also did well in class, though the English language was her major problem. Work too was lighter there compared to the other orphanage. All the children had to attend school and were only required to do work early in the morning and in the evenings.

Marina sometimes missed the orphanage whose rustic life she had sort of got used to. She particularly missed Father Marcel, especially his gentle way of handling the orphans. She also missed Stella Maris who had become her closest friend and confidante by the time she left. As for Sister Bernadette, Marina remembered her with a mixture of respect and fear, though she could not deny that she missed her motherly discipline.

Her heart missed a beat whenever she remembered that Christmas Day and what Matayo had done to her. She had not told a soul about the shameful incident; not even her closest friend, Stella Maris. She had been relieved when Father Marcel had informed her that she would be leaving the orphanage to go to Hoima. At least she would not have to see Matayo's face with that deceptive smile every morning.

Matayo had betrayed her trust. She had begun to believe in him and confide in him. In a funny way, he had reminded her of her dead father. But Marina was determined to put the past behind her. She had no intentions of going back to the orphanage as she had promised Father Marcel. Her new home was now Hoima and she would begin her new life there.

But Matayo had opened her eyes to the world. She would never trust any man again, just like she had vowed not to trust anyone when she had found out that Chantal had betrayed not only her mother's trust, but that of the entire family.

Sister Bernadette visited Marina often whenever she went to Hoima.

She was impressed by what she saw. Marina had blossomed into a full woman, and the baby fat around her cheeks was gone. She had even grown taller within the three months of leaving the orphanage. Her skin was lighter and smoother. Her hair too was longer because the girls in Hoima were allowed to plait and even hot-comb their hair on Sundays.

Father Marcel always inquired about Marina's health on Sister Bernadette's return from Hoima. "How is my little orphan, Marina?" he would ask Sister Bernadette

"She is no longer a little girl, Father, she is now a young woman."

"Is she okay, otherwise?"

"Yes, Father, she couldn't look finer. You should go there and visit her too, she always inquires about you."

And when Father Marcel visited Hoima, he went to see Marina at the convent where she lived with the nuns and the other orphans. "My, Marina, you look great!" Father Marcel exclaimed when he saw her. "What are they feeding you on here? It must be honey and sugar!"

"No, Father," Marina laughed. "It must be the new environment which agrees with my body."

"Sure, sure," Father Marcel agreed. "You are even taller. And how many kilos have you gained? Ten, fifteen," Father Marcel teased her.

"It can't be that much, Father," Marina smiled happily. "I am a bit fatter though than I was at the orphanage. But I can't be that big!"

Father Marcel left a happy man. It was good to see Marina was happy at last. She had come a long way. The teacher had also assured him that she was doing quite well in her studies. Who knows, Father Marcel thought to himself, maybe after there I could send her to the city to attend secondary school.

During the holidays, Marina did not return to the orphanage as she had promised. Father Marcel felt a tinge of disappointment. He had actually intended to show off Marina to the community at the parish. But he knew Marina was fine so he did not worry much. Maybe she had decided to come during third term holidays.

When third term was due to begin, Father Marcel sent Sister Bernadette to go and visit Marina. "We never visited her the whole of second term," he told her. "It's high time we checked on her and asked her if she wishes to spend the holiday, and even have Christmas with us," he added happily.

"I am sure she is all right, Father. Those nuns are good to her. Besides, they would have contacted us if she needed anything."

"I know, Sister, but you know Marina is our responsibility; she belongs here with us," Father Marcel insisted.

"All right, I will go there next week," Sister Bernadette agreed reluctantly. She did understand Father Marcel's special attachment to those orphans he had brought from Rwanda, especially Marina; they were like precious glass to him.

Sister Bernadette went to check on Marina the following week. If the change she had seen in Marina the last time she was there had surprised her, what she saw now shocked her. The girl was all blown up and it was impossible to imagine that she was only fifteen years old.

"Marina!" Sister Bernadette exclaimed. "My goodness, what are you people eating here? No wonder you don't want to come back to our poor orphanage."

"It's not that, Sister," Marina answered. She felt guilty for not going to the orphanage for holidays. But then, Sister Bernadette and Father Marcel would never understand her reasons.

"I will come for Christmas," she lied. "How is Father Marcel and the rest?" she asked, quickly changing the topic.

"They are all fine and send their greetings," Sister Bernadette replied. "But...Marina..." Sister Bernadette said uncertainly, her face lined with worry. "I...you...I mean you are so fat!" Sister Bernadette said in confusion. She looked at Marina more closely. Her breasts were enlarged and...a bell rang in her head.

My God, she thought, horrified, it must be my imagination running away with me.

Marina was staring at Sister Bernadette in confusion.

"What is it, Sister, why are you looking at me like that?" she asked, trying to cover up her own confusion. Maybe confusion was not the right word. She was getting disturbed by the heaviness and movements in her stomach of late. But she had no one to confide in.

"Ah...where is the Mother Superior? I would like to see her and give her a message from Father Marcel," Sister Bernadette said instead.

"I will see if she is around," Marina replied quickly, wanting to get away from Sister Bernadette's stare. As she walked away, Sister Bernadette closed her eyes and said a silent prayer: 'Please God, let it not be what I'm thinking'.

"The Mother Superior is free and she says you can go into her office now," Marina told Sister Bernadette when she came back.

Sister Bernadette walked to the Mother Superior's office. She was quite shaken and dreaded talking to the Mother Superior about what was going on in her mind.

The Mother Superior was also shocked by Sister Bernadette's ashen face. "Are you sick?" she asked her by way of greeting.

Sister Bernadette sank in the chair opposite the Mother Superior's and sighed.

"What is it, Sister, do you come with bad news?" the Mother Superior asked, pushing back her chair to come and stand in front of Sister Bernadette.

Still Sister Bernadette did not say anything. Her hands were shaking and her lower lip trembled.

"Jesus!" the Mother Superior said, now truly alarmed. "Tell me, what is the bad news you bring?" she asked, her voice rising.

"It's Marina," Sister Bernadette blurted out.

"Marina?" the Mother Superior frowned. "I don't understand, has Marina told you that there's something wrong with her? She looks fine to me and..."

"Exactly that!" Sister Bernadette cut her short. "That's what I mean; she looks too fine, or too fat, I mean. And...and...it worries me," Sister Bernadette ended in a whisper.

The Mother Superior went back to her chair, and, heaving a big sigh of relief, sat back heavily.

"Sister Bernadette, could you please explain to me what you mean?" she asked now in her authoritative and formal voice.

"I...I am sorry...Mother Superior, when I saw Marina, I...I thought there was something wrong with her."

"Like what, Sister?" the Mother Superior asked, her voice full of steel.

"Like....Like....she could be pregnant!" Sister Bernadette blurted out. "She...looks so fat."

The Mother Superior stared at her in disbelief. "Marina? Pregnant? That cannot be. Did you talk to her about it?"

"No, I thought I should talk to you first."

"Very well, that was wise of you," she said, her voice laced with sarcasm. "I will call Marina now and ask her."

"I...don't think that's the right way to do it," Sister Bernadette panicked. "Suppose...suppose...it is not true?"

"Then you will tell us how you got that funny idea in your head, Sister," the Mother Superior said in a tough voice.

Chapter Eleven

Sister Bernadette got out of the old ramshackle car which the nuns used when going to Hoima. It had been a donation from the Mother Superior in Hoima and it puffed out thick black smoke as it moved on the potholed murram road from Hoima to the orphanage. But Sister Bernadette was thankful all the same. Before they got that old vehicle, they had to wait for Father Marcel to give them a lift or simply walk the seven kilometres to the main road and then hitch-hike to Hoima.

Her legs felt crumpled and her whole body weary. The scene in Mother Superior's office swept through her mind. Marina had been called in and the Mother Superior had put the question bluntly to her. "Are you pregnant?" she had asked her without any preamble.

Sister Bernadette had looked at Marina's shocked face and immediately knew she had made a grave mistake. Marina had broken into uncontrollable tears and stared at the two nuns in disbelief. The Mother Superior too, had looked uncomfortable and tried to retract her statement.

"Why...why...do you say that?" Marina had asked the two nuns between sobs.

"I...I...was mistaken. When I saw how fat you were, I thought...that maybe you were pregnant," Sister Bernadette said in embarrassment.

The Mother Superior looked from Marina to Sister Bernadette. Her eyes came back to Marina again. She looked at her breasts; they were enlarged; her waist-line had also disappeared. The Mother Superior could not believe it; the girl seemed to have blown up in the past week or so that she had not seen her.

"Marina," she asked quietly," when did you have your last menstrual period?"

Marina seemed unprepared for the question. She gaped at the Mother Superior before answering, "I think not since I came to live here."

The two nuns exchanged knowing looks.

"All right, Marina, you can leave us for a moment," the Mother Superior said at length. Marina walked slowly out of the office.

"What do you think?" the Mother Superior asked.

"I don't know," Sister Bernadette replied quietly, her initial fears returning. "I can bet that girl never slept with a man when she was still at the orphanage. She was never out of my sight!"

"And she has spent here only six months. If she is pregnant, it must be more than six months," the Mother Superior said. "We shall have her examined properly tomorrow at the hospital. Meanwhile, we can ask our nurse to tell us what she thinks."

When the nurse came in the office, the Mother Superior briefed her about their suspicions.

"And you say she has never slept with a man?" the nurse inquired.

" Positive," Sister Bernadette answered.

" Let me talk to her and see what she has to say," the nurse said, moving out of the office and going to talk to Marina who was seated in the living room. When she came back, the nurse's face was lined with worry.

" I don't understand it myself. The girl swears she has never slept with a man and," the nurse continued, "I believe her."

"So what do you make of all this?" the Mother Superior asked her.

"I suspect that she could be suffering from Dysfunctional Uterine Bleeding, a condition which causes irregularities in the menstrual cycle. It occurs mostly in young people who have just begun their menstrual periods. But still, it does not cause weight gain and..."

"As I said before," the Mother Superior said, "we shall have her properly examined tomorrow in hospital: if it's bad news we shall let you know."

"All right," Sister Bernadette said. "I guess I'd better be going back. It's getting late and the car has poor lights." The Mother Superior did not reply. She seemed engrossed in her own thoughts. Sister Bernadette moved out of the office and looked around for Marina to say goodbye, but didn't see her. She didn't want to be caught in the dark with a car without lights and so decided to go without bidding Marina goodbye.

She didn't tell Father Marcel what had transpired in Hoima. There was no need for alarming the ailing priest unduly.

A week later, however, Sister Bernadette was to regret why she had not mentioned anything to Father Marcel, at least to prepare him for the devastating news she had just received.

Marina was not only pregnant but she was in labour, and worse still, the delivery had turned into a difficult one and the Mother Superior feared she might not pull through.

Father Marcel almost collapsed when he heard the news. His whole body trembled and his eyes misted over. Sister Bernadette tried to persuade him to remain behind while she and Stella Maris went to Hoima, but Father Marcel would not hear of it. "I have to be there by her side. She needs me now more than she has ever done before," he kept on saying.

" He will have become another patient by the time we reach Hoima," Sister Bernadette predicted. "Matayo, let's go together so that you can help me with him," Sister Bernadette said, pointing to Father Marcel.

Matayo's face was wan with fear. He too had been shocked by the news about Marina. His voice quivered as he answered, "All right."

No one said a word as they travelled to Hoima, squeezed in Father Marcel's small car. Matayo was at the wheel and Father Marcel sat next to him. Sister Bernadette and Stella Maris were squeezed in the back seat. By the time they covered the thirty four kilometres to Hoima, it was already getting dark. They went straight to the main hospital where Marina was admitted.

The Mother Superior was sitting in the small waiting room with two other nuns and two children from the orphanage in Hoima. Her eyes were red from crying.

"How...is...she?" Father Marcel asked uncertainly. He dreaded the answer the Mother Superior was going to give him.

"She is in bad shape, Father," the Mother Superior answered quietly. "I am sorry I took so long to contact you, but it is a bit difficult to get a message to you with no public transport coming to your place."

Father Marcel nodded in understanding. "Can I see her now?" he asked impatiently.

"I'm not sure, male visitors are not normally allowed in delivery rooms, but I will talk to the doctor and see," the Mother Superior replied, getting up to go and talk to the doctor. A few minutes later, she beckoned to Father Marcel to follow her. Sister Bernadette followed closely. They entered the delivery room in silence. Marina lay on the small delivery bed, covered with a surgical sheet. Her eyes were closed but one could see that her face was contorted in pain. Two nurses and a doctor stood by her. Father Marcel moved closer to the bed and took

67

Marina's warm hands in his.

"Marina," he whispered, but there was no response. Father Marcel continued holding her hand and talking softly to her, but Marina didn't give any indication that she was aware of his presence. As the Father watched, Marina was attacked by a violent spasm of labour pains. She writhed and cried out in pain. The spasms did not last long, and after a few minutes she lay quiet again. The doctor came and checked her pulse.

"She has passed out," he said, "the pain is becoming too much for her."

Father Marcel turned and looked at Sister Bernadette who had remained standing by the door. "Let's go and pray," he said, with a catch in his voice. His face was white with fear.

"She will be all right, Father," the doctor said soothingly, but Father Marcel did not seem to hear.

They moved out of the delivery room and rejoined the others in the small waiting room. Father Marcel did not say anything, but continued to the door leading outside and let himself out. Sister Bernadette told the others about Marina's worsening condition, then went outside to find Father Marcel.

"There is a chapel at the extreme end of the hospital, maybe we can go there and pray," Sister Bernadette suggested. Still Father Marcel did not say anything but continued walking to the chapel Sister Bernadette had pointed out.

They entered the dark chapel. Sister Bernadette groped for the switch and the light flooded the small chapel. Father Marcel looked around, not sure what to do. His eyes landed on a small book shelf in the corner of the church near the piano. He approached the book shelf and leafed through the few books on it. They were covered with dust. He did not know what he was particularly looking for, maybe he only wanted to busy himself as he thought of how to begin a prayer for Marina. Then he saw a big book marked 'Saints.' He opened it with shaky hands. There were dates beside every Saint's name. He turned the pages till he reached September 3rd, with the name 'Rosaria' on the page.

"Let's pray to Saint Rosaria to intercede for Marina," he whispered to Sister Bernadette. They knelt down and prayed. His hands trembled as he brought them together in prayer. After a while, Sister Bernadette stood up and then slowly moved out of the chapel. Father Marcel followed her outside.

"Let's go back," Sister Bernadette suggested, and they went back to the waiting room. It was empty.

"Where is everybody?" Father Marcel asked of no one in particular, his voice filled with fear. He moved to the door leading to the delivery room and it was crowded with the people who had been in the waiting room.

Matayo turned and looked their way, then beckoned them to enter. Father Marcel entered first, not knowing what to expect. Then he looked at Marina still lying on the small delivery bed. Beside her lay a small infant swathed in warm sheets. Father Marcel moved closer and stared at the baby; its huge eyes stared at the world it had just come into, its hair a tangle of black. He lightly touched its skin; it had a chocolate brown complexion and it was as soft as velvet. Father Marcel looked closer at the breath-taking infant; it was big, far too big to have been delivered by Marina who was just a child herself.

"Welcome into the world, Rosaria," he said softly, his eyes filling with tears. He now turned and looked at Marina, who seemed to have fallen into a deep sleep. He touched her forehead. It was warm and covered with perspiration. He wiped away some of the sweat from her forehead.

The doctor was staring at him strangely. "Father, had you already chosen a name for the baby? How did you know it would be a girl?" he asked him.

Father Marcel smiled through his tears and answered, "Today is Saint Rosaria's feast day, and we prayed to her to intercede for Marina."

Marina opened her eyes briefly and looked at the people around her; she seemed not to know where she was. Stella Maris was instantly at her side. But Marina closed her eyes again and the doctor informed them that she needed to get a lot of rest.

"I think you can now wait outside," he said to the small group in the delivery room.

They did not go far, they went back to the waiting room to await news about Marina's condition. Matayo glanced at his watch. It was past two in the morning. "Father, you need to have some rest," he said in a concerned voice. "I suggest you go to the Father's residence and rest; I will inform you if there's any change in Marina's condition."

Father Marcel did not reply. It was obvious that he was not going anywhere until Marina was out of danger. They spent the few hours to day- break lying in the chairs in the waiting room. At six o'clock, Marina was still unconscious. The Mother Superior and the two nuns went back to the convent to make coffee and when they came back, they

69

were informed that Marina had regained consciousness and was now out of danger.

Marina was transferred from the delivery room to the maternity ward that morning. Stella Maris and Sister Bernadette were standing by her bed, but neither of them knew what to say. Marina was still feeling groggy and could manage to say only very little. When they moved out, Father Marcel went in; he wanted to see Marina alone.

"How are you feeling now?" he asked gently.

"I am better," Marina answered, averting her eyes.

"And the little one; how is she?"

Marina turned and looked at the baby who lay beside her but she did not answer. Father Marcel moved to the baby's side and gingerly touched her little fingers. She looked angelic in her sleep.

"How are you, Rosaria?" he whispered to her. He sat on the bed and took Marina's hands in his. Her eyes were wet with tears as she looked up at Father Marcel, with guilt written all over her face.

"Marina, it does you no good to cry now. You are still weak and you need to get better soon." Father Marcel's gentle voice brought more tears to her eyes. How could she ever explain how she felt right now. Father Marcel let her cry awhile, then spoke again. "There's no need to cry, Marina. You ought to be proud!"

Marina shook her head, more tears welling up in her eyes. "I don't love her, Father," she confessed, closing her eyes, not wanting to see the shock in Father Marcel's eyes.

"It's all right," Father Marcel said. "It's understandable. You have gone through a lot, but with time, you will get used to having Rosaria around you."

Marina noted that Father Marcel had avoided using the words ' love Rosaria'. At least he understood how she felt.

"Thank you," she said.

Father Marcel squeezed her fingers and nodded.

"We have decided to take Rosaria with us. She will stay with us at the orphanage until you get better and you are able to join us," Father Marcel said. He had not discussed it with anybody yet, but he knew it was the logical thing to do. "You will stay with Stella Maris who will help you," he continued. " If you need anything you can send her to tell us."

Marina was quiet. She held on to Father Marcel's hand, not wanting him to go. Suddenly, she was terrified of being left alone. She began crying again.

"It's okay, Marina, everything will be all right," Father Marcel assured her. But his own eyes were not quite dry. He looked at Marina and remembered that day in Rwanda when she had wandered into the camp. At that time, she looked so vulnerable and frightened, just like she did now.

He took the baby in his arms and held her out to Marina. "Would you like to hold her for a moment before we take her?" he asked.

Marina looked at the child she had brought into the world and felt nothing. She shook her head slowly.

"It's okay," Father Marcel whispered. "We have to go back now," he said as he stood up. "We shall keep in touch," he continued, avoiding looking at her because he knew she was crying again. He moved quickly to the door and let himself out.

When he told the doctor what he had decided to do, the latter was sceptical. "How can you manage to look after a one-day old-baby, Father?" he asked, surprised.

"We do it all the time, Doctor," Father Marcel answered smiling. "Sister Bernadette will buy some more feeding bottles and we shall begin feeding Rosaria on cow's milk. Until her mother is able to join us," he added. The doctor nodded doubtfully.

Matayo was already seated in the car when Father Marcel got there. "Is Marina coming with us?" he asked bewildered.

"No. Why?" Father Marcel asked.

"Ah...the baby..." Matayo said pointing at the baby in Father Marcel's arms.

"Yes, the baby is coming with us but the mother is remaining behind," Father Marcel answered.

"I...see," Matayo said, relief washing over him. He had avoided seeing Marina that morning. He was still in a state of shock and did not know what he would have said to her.

Chapter Twelve

Marina was released from the hospital three weeks later. She did not go back to the orphanage, but went to live with the Mother Superior at the Hoima convent, together with Stella Maris who was supposed to help her recuperate.

The two girls were still friends, but they never talked much. Marina had withdrawn into herself and she was depressed. She talked only when talked to. Stella Maris had once asked her how she had got pregnant and who Rosaria's father was. Marina had stared at her friend strangely and after that, she had spent two days without talking to her.

Physically, Marina had healed though she had lost a lot of weight. But she was just impossible to live with. When she was not sulking, she was brooding, and only snapped at people when she tried to talk. Stella Maris wished they were back at the orphanage, and everything was normal again. But Marina had already hinted that she would never go back to that orphanage, but wanted to go away somewhere where nobody knew her to begin a new life.

Stella Maris remembered how Marina had been obsessed with leaving the orphanage that time after Christmas. She had pestered Father Marcel until he had to send her to Hoima to start studying. It was the same now. She wanted to go away, but where? Not even she knew.

Stella Maris often talked to the Mother Superior about Marina's mood swings. "I don't know if she will ever talk again," Stella Maris said sadly. "She is so withdrawn and sad."

"I don't know either," the Mother Superior said. "Maybe I will talk to the doctor and see if he has any medicine for depression." But the doctor assured her that Marina would come out of it herself. "It was a shock even to herself, the poor girl didn't even know that she was pregnant," the doctor said. "And the experience she went through was traumatic."

Father Marcel had visited them twice but every time he began to talk about Rosaria's progress, Marina's face would fall. She had no desire to know how her child was. Father Marcel was disappointed. He had hoped that after some months, Marina would begin feeling some motherly love for her daughter. He was ready to give her more time. Maybe it was still too early.

Sister Bernadette also came to visit them. She looked at Marina and knew what the girl was going through. She needed some counselling but she doubted if that would get her out of her depression. She needed somebody who would talk to her, somebody who had ever felt like she did now.

"Marina, look at yourself, you act as if what happened to you means the end of the world. You are only sixteen and you still have your whole life ahead of you," she tried to reason with her.

" It's the end of the world for me!" Marina burst out furiously. "I have no future any more: I can't go back to school, I lost respect among my friends, I..."

" No, Marina, you still have your life and..."

"My whole life is shattered," Marina was now shouting. "Somebody shattered it when he raped me and..." She stopped herself before she could say any more.

"Who was it, Marina?" Sister Bernadette asked gently, not wanting to lose this moment when Marina seemed to have opened up.

Marina was crying, the memories of that fateful Christmas Day and the pain she had gone through coming back to her. But if she ever wanted to confide in anyone, certainly it would not be Sister Bernadette. What did a nun know about rape and childbirth.

"Tell me, Marina. I will understand," Sister Bernadette coaxed her gently. Marina wiped the tears but did not say any more.

"All right", Sister Bernadette said. "I will tell you how much I have suffered myself, then you can know that you are not alone."

" Suffered?" Marina echoed.

"Yes, my dear, I have suffered a lot in this world. You see, my parents always regarded me as a disgrace to them," Sister Bernadette began, a faraway look in her eyes. "They thought I was the cursed one because I was the ugliest among the three daughters and at thirty, I was not yet married. When my father wanted to go for an important appointment, he never wanted to meet me because I would bring him bad luck." Sister Bernadette laughed bitterly before she continued.

"He would tell my younger sister to stand in the door way so that he would meet her as he went out. That way, he was assured of good luck. My mother never allowed me to serve sauce during meals because 'I had a bad hand which made sauce go bad', she would say.

"If I served sauce and some of it remained in the saucepan, by morning it would have gone bad, simply because I touched it. And my grandmother," Sister Bernadette continued in the same flat voice, "never allowed me to rub medicine on her aching joints because again 'I had a bad hand which never cured'. I was considered the unlucky one. If somebody gave me a goat, it would die in childbirth. So it went without saying that at thirty, I had failed to find myself a husband. I resorted to prayer," Sister Bernadette continued.

"I prayed to God to give me a husband, for hadn't Jesus said 'Ask and you will be given?" I particularly prayed to the Holy Virgin Mary to intercede for me. I even secured a statue of the Virgin Mary and placed it on a separate table with fresh flowers beside it. I went to church three times a day and in the evening, I joined the nuns reciting the Rosary. The church was the pivot of my life."

She had been talking rapidly, but fell silent for a moment. Marina looked at her and there was sadness in her eyes. She began seeing the person she had once thought of as emotionless, in a new light.

"After I had prayed for a year, I finally met him," Sister Bernadette continued. "He was a young handsome man who had been posted to the school where I taught. He was much younger than me and I thought I was too ugly for him. But he fell in love with me at first sight.

"He assured me that beauty should not be judged by what a woman looked like, but rather the way a woman behaved, walked and smiled. That made her beautiful. I believed him. I was happy, Marina; for the first time in my life, I was a happy woman," Sister Bernadette said with a light in her eyes. "I took him to meet my parents and I will never forget the shock on their faces. 'Where did you get such a handsome man from?' their expression seemed to say. As a sign of gratitude, I placed a new bouquet beside the Virgin Mary's statue in my bedroom. Three months later I was pregnant."

" Pregnant!", Marina could not hide her shock.

"Yes, Marina, I was pregnant," Sister Bernadette repeated.

"But...I don't...understand, Sister," Marina said uncertainly. "What happened then?"

"A lot , Marina, a lot happened," Sister Bernadette sighed. "First of all, I was ecstatic. 'God is indeed great,' I remember thinking. 'A husband

and a child all in one year!' My second thought was that we had to get married right away. I did not want my parents to scorn me for 'living in sin', and I knew that if the authorities at the school where we taught came to learn of my pregnancy, the headmaster would chase us away. You see, it was a church-founded school and they were obsessed with upholding morals. A single mother would not be a good example to the young girls in the school," Sister Bernadette explained. "I told him that."

"What was his name?" Marina interrupted.

"David," Sister Bernadette replied. She glanced at Marina sharply. "Why are you interested in his name, anyway?"

Marina shrugged and smiled uncomfortably.

"All right," Sister Bernadette said, not pressing for an answer. "As I was saying, I told David that I was pregnant. He was not as thrilled as I was. Actually, he said something about not knowing what to do. I then suggested that we could get married right away." That's when he threw the bombshell, Marina, and it landed right on my head, shattering my whole life. He was already married," he told me, and said he had never intended our relationship to become so serious. I..."Sister Bernadette could not continue as sobs were choking her. Marina held her hand to comfort her. There was a lot of pain in her eyes.

She must still be living with the pain after all these years, Marina thought sympathetically.

"I was mad," Sister Bernadette continued, regaining her composure. "I wanted to murder him. I have no recollection of how I eventually reached home. I lay on the bed and could not even cry. My eyes finally fell on the statue of the Blessed Virgin Mary. 'Even you, solace of desperate cases, you betrayed me! Just like David!' I remember thinking bitterly. I got hold of the statue and was about to smash it against the wall when I heard a knock at the door. The door was ajar and I peeped through it. tall man was standing there and his silhouette resembled David's. It was dark outside and I could not see properly. In my blind rage, however, I thought it was David. What is this liar doing here in my house, I wondered. With all the energy I could muster, I hurled the statue squarely at the man's head." Marina flinched, the anger in Sister Bernadette's eyes frightening her.

"I had hit the wrong man," Sister Bernadette was saying. " I rushed to the door to see how hurt the man was. He was writhing in pain and when I tried to touch him, he kicked me hard in the stomach, thinking I was going to hit him again. He must have thought I was a lunatic." Sister Bernadette laughed drily. "Anyway," she continued, "that kick must have

75

had so much fear , anger and I don't know what else, behind it. I clutched my stomach as I felt something turn inside me. I remember my vision blurring and I felt dizzy before I passed out."

Sister Bernadette was silent as she remembered something which had happened to her more than thirty years ago. Marina, too, fell silent. She did not want to say anything which would disrupt Sister Bernadette's narration.

"I woke up in a hospital," she continued, "and the first thought which came to mind was that I was dead, and I was in heaven among angels because everywhere I looked was white. I had lost the baby, the doctor later informed me. I felt empty, though somehow I remember feeling a great sense of relief.

"The man I had hit had taken me to a private hospital, thinking that I was going to die. His name was Martin, I later found out. He had come to my house to ask for directions to his friend's house who taught at our school." Sister Bernadette sighed before she continued, "After that, he came to see me every day and we developed a special relationship. Like me, he was estranged from his family and had never had anything to call his own.

"He was single and childless. I didn't love him and knew that I never would. But at least he was there for me and at that time, I needed him. I felt rejected and useless. I had lost trust in everyone, even God. I felt like going away somewhere where nobody knew me and starting my life all over." Sister Bernadette looked at Marina, and the latter averted her eyes. They both knew that was exactly how Marina felt right now.

"Martin was ready to offer me a new life and he was willing to accept me as I was," Sister Bernadette continued. "When I was discharged from hospital, I moved in with him. He was a shy man and he did not approach me sexually for a long time. He only cooked and fussed over me. I was living in a trance. I only ate and slept. I refused to think of the past, present or future. Life had lost its meaning for me and I was only existing, not living. Martin was an understanding man. He gave me time and waited until I got out of my depression.

"After about two years, I got pregnant again and nine months later I gave birth to twins - boys."

"You...have...children, Sister Bernadette?" Marina stammered in disbelief.

"Why don't you let me finish my story, Marina? Just be patient and you will know everything in good time," Sister Bernadette answered evasively.

"Okay, continue," Marina said containing her impatience.

"The twins looked like their father. Luckily they had not inherited any of my ugly features."

Marina grimaced. Whenever Sister Bernadette mentioned the word 'ugly', she just spat it out. Marina felt sorry for her, for whoever had planted the idea in her that she was ugly had made her whole life miserable. She remembered what the girls at the orphanage called her, especially after she had punished them: *balikitwe*, referring to her misshapen head or *biguru bey'enjojo*, referring to her big legs and heavy gait.

"I was almost content with what life had offered me," Sister Bernadette was talking again. "An adoring husband and two children. God was merciful after all, I thought. But God is like a parent, I remember the priest telling us often, he only gives you what he thinks is best for you.

"Every evening," Sister Bernadette continued, "Martin took me and the twins for a ride. The children had made him a happy man and I was glad that I had given him that gift. One evening, I was not feeling well and I did not accompany them on the evening ride.

"I started getting worried when by ten o'clock they had not returned. Normally, the ride ended by nine o'clock. By midnight I was getting frantic and I rang the police. Later, the police called back to say that my husband and children had been involved in an accident and they were all dead."

"Oh no," Marina cried. "It ...must...have...been...been..." she tried to find the right word, "terrible!" she finally said.

"Yes," Sister Bernadette said without emotion. Time had healed the pain she felt then and she could now talk about the incident without feeling the terrible pain she had felt that day. But she still remembered how she had felt: numb with shock, then disbelief, thinking that the police could be playing games with her. The truth of the accident had dawned on her after she had looked at the three bodies. That's when she had decided to end her life. She had slashed her wrists with a brand new razor. At that time she felt nothing, not even pain, maybe a little remorse at what she was doing.

She had woken up in a hospital again but this time instead of white, there was filth everywhere. It was a small hospital run by nuns and they treated people who could not afford treatment at private hospitals.

That day, a white priest had come to visit the sick in the hospital. He reached her bed and took her hands in his. "My daughter, why did you try to end your precious life?' he had asked her quietly.

"Precious?" she had echoed. "It's not precious, Father," she had answered.

The priest had smiled at her and said, "Yes it is, my daughter. You only need to make it happy and worthwhile.'"

"I have never been happy in my life, Father, maybe once...when I had . a man...and...now..." She had failed to continue.

"You could become Christ's bride," the priest had said to her. "He is very dependable and will never let you down. He won't even die!"

"Christ's bride? How?" Bernadette had asked in a dull voice.

"You could become a nun. You could come back with me to the parish and I will make you happy."

"Sister," Marina broke into her reverie.

The events of that day had come back with such intensity that Sister Bernadette had to shake her head several times to clear it.

"Yes, Marina, I was devastated. That's when I decided to become a nun, and find everlasting peace as Father Marcel had told me. But all that is in the past. I left the hospital and went to the parish with Father Marcel where I became a nun. Since then, I have never looked back."

Silence fell between them. Sister Bernadette had a dazed look in her eyes and she seemed to be engrossed in thoughts she had had no room for in her heart for the past thirty years.

Marina had been mesmerised by the whole story and was yet to comprehend the gist of it all.

"Did...did you attain the happiness you were seeking?" Marina asked in a whisper.

"It doesn't matter now. What matters is that I managed to put the past behind me and start a new life. And that is what you need to do now, start a new life."

"But I want to be happy," Marina said, her voice taking on a childish edge.

"I know, Marina, it's very important, but it's more important to put everything behind you," Sister Bernadette answered, knowing she was now talking to the 'child' in Marina.

"I also want to go away where they don't know me," Marina continued, sobbing quietly.

"I will arrange that, Marina, just be patient. But in the meantime, I want you to start living your own life," Sister Bernadette said. "Promise?"

"I promise, Sister," Marina said, a smile appearing on her mouth and spreading slowly to her eyes. She was already beginning to feel good.

Chapter Thirteen

Sister Bernadette did keep her promise. She was determined to send Marina away to give her the chance she needed to begin a new life. Families from the city usually came to the orphanage to pick the older girls and take them as domestic maids. The girls at the orphanage had a good record of hard work and upright morals. Sister Bernadette was there to see to that.

But she did not want to give Marina away as a housemaid. She needed her to stay with a family which would offer her the security and protection she needed to start a new life. Such families were not easy to come by; no one in the city wanted to take on an extra mouth to feed in return for nothing.

Sister Bernadette came across the ideal family by chance. Mr and Mrs Magezi hailed from the village just next to where the orphanage was. They normally came to the village to celebrate Christmas and New Year. They would pray in the small church at the parish and afterwards linger around the compound to greet the people they had not seen in the past year.

This particular Christmas, Mr Magezi had been sent by one of the priests of Mbuya Catholic parish to deliver some medicine to Father Marcel. The Magezi family prayed in Mbuya when they were in the city and the Verona Fathers there knew them well. Father Marcel's health was deteriorating with each passing day. That Christmas, he had not even managed to go to church to celebrate Mass, something he had always cherished in his healthier days. This prompted Sister Bernadette to go and check on him immediately Mass was over. And there she met Mr Magezi. Father Marcel introduced him to her and was full of praises for Mr. and Mrs Magezi who were good Christians, kind and charitable. After Mr Magezi had left, an idea occurred to Sister Bernadette.

"Father, what do you think of Marina going to live with the Magezis? They sound like the people I have been searching for," Sister Bernadette said excitedly.

Father Marcel pondered for a moment. "As far as I know, they are good people, the Verona Fathers at Mbuya know them quite well. They also say that Mr magezi is a very well known and influential lawyer. Talk to him and see what he says," Father Marcel concluded.

Sister Bernadette saw the Magezis the following day when they came for the Thanksgiving Mass. She talked to them and made an appointment to meet them later that day.

When they met, Sister Bernadette explained Marina's plight to them and how she needed to go someplace else. They were very sympathetic and understanding.

"Unfortunately, we don't need another extra hand right now," Mrs Magezi said regretfully. "We already have two housemaids!"

"We don't have a big family and the house work is really light," the husband added.

"I assume all the kids are grown up and living on their own now," Sister Bernadette said, trying to cover her disappointment.

"Not really," Mr Magezi answered, shifting in his chair uncomfortably

"And...I didn't mean for Marina to be a housemaid, I would prefer her to be more of a...I mean I want a safe place for her so that she can be given the chance to start life anew," Sister Bernadette tried to explain further.

"We understand, Sister," Mr Magezi said gently. "I shall think it over with my wife and shall let you know. You can also show us the girl so we can talk to her."

"All right," Sister Bernadette replied, relieved. At least they had not let her down completely. "But...ah...the girl, I mean, Marina is not here with us, she now lives in Hoima," Sister Bernadette said, her initial fear returning. She knew she would never get Marina to come back to the orphanage in time.

Mr Magezi thought for a moment. "We usually pass via Hoima when going back to the city. We shall drop by the orphanage and see her." He smiled at the Sister in reassurance.

After Sister Bernadette had left, Magezi's wife turned to him. "You didn't mean any of that, did you? We don't need people crowding our house," her tone was laced with anger.

"Of course not," her husband replied, "I had to say something to please the old nun; she doesn't know the burdens of feeding many people in the city."

Sister Bernadette could not wait to break the good news to Father Marcel.

"They have agreed to pass by the orphanage in Hoima and see Marina; if they like her, they might take her," she said with elation .

"That would be good for Marina," Father Marcel said, equally happy. "I will give them a message for the Mother Superior; some official and urgent letter. And I will send Marina a photograph of Rosaria, the one I took recently. I think she would like to look at it."

When the Magezis went to bid Father Marcel farewell, he gave them the two messages he had already prepared. They looked uncomfortable and he was quick to say, "If it's inconveniencing you, then I will dispatch my boy, Matayo to take them. They are rather urgent and..."

"We shall take them, Father," Mr Magezi said quickly. He could not refuse the ailing Father anything; he had done a lot for the local community; at least he owed him one small favour.

"Thank you," Father Marcel said, "and I hope...I...everything works out fine." He had been about to say, 'you treat Marina well' but he remembered they had not decided whether they were taking her or not. Not until they saw her.

They reached Hoima town and went straight to the orphanage which was located at the convent, about two kilometres out of town. They met the Mother Superior and gave her the two messages from Father Marcel.

"I can see this is for Marina, let me call her so that you can give it to her personally."

"No," they said in unison.

"It's okay, you can give it to her." Mrs Magezi added.

" She is right here; besides, she would like to know how Father Marcel is faring," the Mother Superior insisted.

Before they could reply, she had walked out of the sitting room and they could hear her calling Marina's name.

Marina came quickly. She looked at the Magezis questioningly.

"They have your message from Father Marcel," the Mother Superior explained. "Here," she handed her the envelope containing the photograph.

"Thank you," Marina said quietly. "How is he?" she asked, her eyes full of compassion.

"He is.weak," Mr Magezi replied. He saw a shadow fall on Marina's face and added quickly, "Not very weak. I think he will be okay."

Mrs Magezi was all along watching Marina. She saw the love in her eyes when she talked of Father Marcel and knew immediately that the two must be very close. She remembered the old nun telling them what Marina had gone through in Rwanda and how Father Marcel had found her and given her a new life at the orphanage. "He is like a father to all of them, especially Marina, whom he has a special attachment to," the nun had told them. And now Father Marcel's health was poor, and Marina was going to be deprived of yet another 'father'. Her heart went out to the poor girl; she was alone in this world. Mrs Magezi looked at her more closely and noticed her sunken eyes. She needs a new life, she thought to herself.

"Shall we?" her husband was talking to her.

"What?" Mrs Magezi snapped back to attention.

"I said let's go now; we still have a long way and..."

"I think we better take Marina with us," Mrs Magezi whispered to her husband, her own eyes filling with tears. "We...can't...just leave her!"

Mr Magezi stared at his wife, momentarily puzzled. "But...I thought..."

"I know what I thought then, but I have changed my mind."

Marina and the Mother Superior looked at the couple in front of them in confusion

"What are you talking about?" the Mother Superior asked them sharply.

"It's about Marina; we want to take her with us and offer her a new life," Mrs Magezi said happily. She was glad she had agreed to pass by the orphanage.

PART TWO

Chapter One

George Walusimbi was a man of slight build. He had tiny deep-set eyes which seemed to disappear in his skull when his forehead furrowed deep in anger, making him look sinister. Whenever he was in a happy mood, he smiled broadly, emphasising the slight dimples on his cheeks, which gave him an almost boyish look. It was almost impossible to reconcile the angry George with the happy one. The two were like two different people. He talked with a slight stammer and walked swiftly as if he was constantly in a hurry.

At first sight, it was difficult to tell George's age. He looked somewhere between twenty five and forty five. He was a man who could easily disappear in a crowd because there was nothing significant about him, nothing that one could remember, unless one was observant enough to notice the stammer in his speech. But this occured only when he was nervous.

He wore stylish, fancy clothes but liked to keep his hair short with an ordinary haircut. He was conscious of his short stature and always wore high-heeled boots.

He also wore photosensitive sunglasses, whether it was night or day and gave one the impression that he was trying to hide his true identity.

Born in 1961 in the Sese Islands on the shores of Lake Victoria,

George was the first born in a family of nine. His parents were poor and consequently could not keep their children in school for long. George dropped out of school at the age of fourteen after completing primary seven.

He was not a person to sit at home wallowing in self-pity over his parents' inability to send him to a secondary school. Neither did he intend to join in the family's fishing business. He had seen what it had done to his father, uncles and cousins: callused hands, working long and queer hours late into the night, waiting for the moon to disappear so that the fish could not see the nets and baits laid out to catch them. And of course the degeneration into alcoholics in order to ward off the stinking odour of fish constantly on their bodies. No, George had decided long ago, that was not the life for him.

He worked briefly cleaning fish for the rich fishermen who came to the island to buy fish for export. That was how he raised enough money to take him away from the filthy island.

George had an uncle, his father's younger brother, who lived in the city. He did not know much about him because his uncle rarely came to the island. Their parents were both dead and Ntambi did not get on well with his less educated and poverty stricken brothers. He regarded their inability to educate their children as sheer laziness and ignorance because he knew they made some good money from fishing but squandered it on booze.

From the little that George knew of his uncle, he was a rich man with a good job, owned a car and a beautiful big house. Somehow, George talked to one of the fishermen who came to the island and who happened to know his uncle well. The fisherman promised to take George to his uncle's place so long as George could pay his own fare. George had saved enough money from cleaning fish and early one morning, they set off in the dilapidated creaking boat which was the only means of transport from the island to the mainland, arriving in the city late in the evening.

Ntambi was a principled, no-nonsense man. His reaching the top ranks in the corporation had been systematic and based on merit. He lived a modest life with his wife and three children. Like most accountants, Ntambi was also meticulous and calculating in every step he took lest he made the wrong move. He was also very orderly and immaculately clean, both at home and in his office.

He viewed his young nephew's arrival as an unnecessary inconvenience in his otherwise orderly lifestyle. Besides, he did not want those relatives from the island to 'contaminate' his children with their uncouth manners. His house was four bed-roomed, one bed room was for the two girls, another for the live-in baby- sitter who shared it with their baby boy; the large room was theirs. The other smaller room was his study.The servants quarters were occupied by their *shamba* boy. Where then would his nephew sleep. When George told him the purpose of his visit, he was appalled. A primary seven drop-out looking for employment in the city! The boy must be crazy.

It was his wife who saved George. She saw how useful the young village boy could be to them. He could take over the duties of their shamba boy and on top of that, collect food from the market, wash their car and even look after the chicks she intended to rear. And all for a little fee. Or nothing at all.

George was undeterred by the chores he was told to do. He was a strong boy used to hard work and he carried out his duties to perfection. He always remembered his mother saying that good things come to those who wait.

After six months of playing house/ errand boy, even his uncle was impressed. He even suggested getting him employment in the Railways Corporation where he worked. George could do the house chores very early in the morning and go to the office to do his office messenger's duties later. That way, he could earn an extra income.

George began to see his dream of becoming rich one day take shape. The small job, however low paying, was a beginning. He saw and admired the mansions he passed by while going to work and visualised owning one like them some day. He dreamt of driving a sleek limousine like the ones some of the bosses at the railway station drove to work.

He wanted to be rich. He had ambition and he believed in the old adage that where there is a will there is a way. The only snag was how he was going to fulfill his ambition, given his low level of education.

He kept his eyes and ears open. Her listened to every conversation when his uncle hosted important people. He read any literature he came by and he was slowly beginning to be knowledgeable in different subjects. He was mostly fascinated with figures. He would sneak into his uncle's study room and stare at the cash books and ledgers and the figures he saw left his mouth dry. The figures were enormous: one hundred million, two hundred million. The mere sight of them made him feel rich and boy, did he like that feeling! It was a sweet feeling. He would roll the figures on his tongue and they tasted great. His heart would beat faster at the mere thought of having that kind of money. George was careful not to let his ambitions show. At work, he was still the humble errand boy and at home, he still performed the duties expected of him. It was also important that he should gain people's trust and confidence, especially those he worked for; that way, he could be considered for promotion.

When the fancy secretaries sent him to buy their lunch, he returned the balance, however small it was. They would offer it to him and he would politely refuse it until they coaxed him into taking it. As a result, at the end of one year, even his boss began entrusting him with large amounts of money to take to the bank and fat cheques to deliver. George would stare at the money in his possession and his whole body would tremble with excitement. How did other people earn so much money? He wished he knew the formula for becoming rich.

Somehow, he associated banks with wealth. He was determined to learn how banks operated and the chance to take money and bank it on the corporation's account was an excellent opportunity. He learnt what it took to open an account and read widely about credit schemes. He did not understand most of the terminology therein but at least he was getting a rough idea of how they operated. He knew that when the time came to become rich, knowledge about banking would come in handy.

His parents were always pestering him to send them money to educate his younger siblings but he turned a deaf ear. He was saving every shilling he made. He would get a lift from home to work and back and also did not spend anything on food and rent.

At the end of two years however, he still had a miserable figure in the envelope he kept tucked away at the bottom of his suitcase. He realised that saving was not the way to richness; there had to be another way and he had to find it.

Chapter Two

George's chance knocked on the door one day after he had been working for three years. His boss had sent him to deliver a cheque to a businessman in Masaka, a big town outside Kampala city, who had supplied stationery to the corporation. The cheque was in a sealed envelope and he did not have a chance of looking at the amount it was worth.

His boss had cautioned him not give it to anyone else except its rightful owner. George spent some time trying to trace the businessman and by the time he located him it was well past six o'clock. The businessman was travelling to the city and offered to give George a lift back.

As George sat in the comfort of the luxurious car, he relaxed in his seat and contemplated driving and owning such a car. He closed his eyes and listened to the humming of the powerful engine. If he were to buy a car, it would be like the one he was sitting in right now, not like the miserable one his uncle owned.

He must have dozed off because he was awakened by a deafening noise and screech of tyres. The car had hit a stationary trailer parked dangerously at a corner. The powerful car swerved and skidded off the road, overturning twice. George closed his eyes and put up his hands instinctively to protect his head. When he opened them, he saw that the car was balancing precariously on one side and one slight movement would bring it down. George glanced at the other occupant in the driver's seat. He was making a funny noise, the steering wheel pressed hard on his chest and blood was oozing from his nostrils and mouth.

Overcoming his own shock, George managed to pull himself out of the car, careful not to upset its balance. Then with all his might he pushed it to a normal position.

The businessman was trying to say something through the foam of blood in his mouth but George could not get what the man was saying. He knew he had to get the man out of the car fast.

He seemed to be in great pain and was gasping for breath. He did not know how he would manage to pull him out without risking injuring him further. The windscreen was smashed and the front part of the car had caved in. The driver's and passenger's doors were all bashed in and could not open. He had to practically pull the injured man by the shoulders and through the window as he gasped in pain.

He succeeded in pulling the man out and they both collapsed on the ground. It was only then that George realised his own injuries and felt the pain. His forearms were badly bruised and there was a big, deep cut on his forehead. There was blood all over him. The businessman was trying to point at the wrecked car. George dragged his aching body back to the car and peered inside. There was a small leather briefcase lying near the driver's seat, unscathed by the accident. George brought it back where the man lay. The man kept on pointing at the car, trying to say something. But it was impossible for him because more blood was oozing from his mouth. As George looked on helplessly, not knowing what to do, the man heaved and gasped, then lay still.

George sat there, all senses numbed by the shock of the accident and the death of the businessman. He could not think properly, his head was throbbing dangerously and he felt his vision blur. Blood spurted out of the cut on his forehead and he knew he had to get help immediately, but still he did not move.

Then his eyes flew to the briefcase now lying next to the dead man. He quickly forced it open and there, lying undisturbed by the impact of the accident, were crisp ten thousand shilling notes. George gaped at the money in total disbelief. He had never seen so much money in his life! Gingerly, he touched the money and his hands shook slightly. His heart pounded fast and he felt a trickle of perspiration run from his injured forehead. On top of the notes, lay the envelope containing the cheque he had delivered to the man. Without knowing why, George removed the envelope, pocketed it and then closed the briefcase.

He felt dizzy and nauseous and knew he was going to collapse if he did not get help soon. As he staggered to the roadside, he heard a deafening sound and automatically turned to look at the wrecked car. It had burst into flames and the fire was already eating up the once beautiful, powerful car.

George was rescued by the Mobile Police Unit which arrived at the scene of the accident an hour later. He dutifully handed over the briefcase to the policeman and told him that it belonged to the dead man. He was driven to hospital and stayed there for a week.

The people George worked and associated with learnt with disbelief how George had surrendered a briefcase full of money to the police!

"He has missed a once-in-a-lifetime opportunity. Poor boy, the village is still in him even after three years of living in the city," his fellow workers commented. "After all, the man was dead, who was going to say there had ever been a briefcase containing money? The car was also burnt." People laughed behind his back.

The corporation compensated George with one hundred thousand shillings to pay the hospital bills. He was praised by his bosses but scorned by his friends and workmates. Others who read about the incident in the papers wrote him off as the most stupid Ugandan they had ever seen. "The little fool must be bananas, he must be bonkers! I wish it were me..." they lamented.

The briefcase, George later learnt, had contained eight million shillings.

George spent one month recuperating. During that time, he planned. He had a cheque in his possession which could easily be converted into cash but he did not know how to do it. He read more about the banking system and how it operated, but did not understand it all. He knew he had to get technical advice, but whom could he trust. Certainly not his uncle or his workmates at the corporation.

On the many occasions he had visited the bank to deposit the corporation's cheques or cash, he had sort of got used to one teller in particular. He did not remember how it had started, but this teller had always been easy for him to approach. Unlike the others whom he heard reprimanding the clients for filling in the deposit forms incorrectly, this one never once shouted at him. Not even during those first days when he had just started going to the bank, and would write the amount in words wrongly, or miss writing the date.

Whenever there was a queue, especially at the end of the month or because the money-counting machines had broken down, she would beckon him to jump the line and come in front.

As he sat now in his room thinking, his mind went to her. She looked kind enough, maybe she would be able to help. He decided to go and talk to her.

At the bank, the queue was light and before he knew it, he was standing in front of her. She extended her hand to take the money she thought he had brought for banking, but he shook his head.

"No, I have not come to deposit money today," he said self-consciously

"Well, what can I do for you?" she smiled at him.

"I...want...nee...eed to tal...aaak to you," George stammered. He was obviously very nervous.

"Sure, what do you wish to talk about?" she asked calmly.

"May...maybe...wee co...ould meeet out...side," the stammer was making it impossible for him to talk. She must have noticed his nervousness because she immediately came to his rescue.

"Look, I'm busy right now, but maybe we can meet over lunch time."

"Where?" he asked excitedly.

She told him and he moved away to let the next client be served.

He was at the arranged venue fifteen minutes before the agreed time. Luckily, she was there on the dot of the hour.

"Well...," she began

"I wanted to show you this," George said, quickly dipping his hand in the pocket and coming out with the cheque.

She examined it carefully before saying anything.

"Where did you get this from?" she asked finally.

"I picked it," George lied.

"And?"

"I...want to turn it into...into cash." The initial fear was gone and he felt some confidence. Maybe it was because of her disarming manner.

"I see," she said quietly. " But it does not belong to you. How do you intend to go about it?"

"I'm not sure, that is...that is why I came to you," George said uncertainly.

"Let me think about it and I will see what can be done," she said, still smiling.

George was surprised at her quick reaction. She didn't seem surprised!

"We could meet here, say tomorrow? Same time? Is that okay with you?"

It was not okay with him. He wanted to know *now* whether it could be turned into cash. But he could not push her.

"Sure," he answered trying to sound light.

She got up abruptly. "Well, I have to go now," she said glancing at her wrist watch..

Before he could say anything, she had already started to walk away. "The cheque," George wanted to scream after her, but she was already out of the door.

Well, he sighed. At least he had tried.

The following day, he was there five minutes to the agreed time. But she did not appear until thirty minutes later. And she was not alone. She had a policeman with her whom she seemed to be well at ease with.

George felt fear grip him. His legs began to buckle under the table and he trembled like a leaf. He felt a bout of dizziness wash over him. She had betrayed him, he thought to himself in disbelief. If only his legs were not trembling he could then flee. She was now almost at the table where he sat and the smile was still there on her face.

"I'm sorry for being so late," she said brightly, "but my brother here came from the village and I had to attend to him first," she added, pointing at the policeman. "I hope you don't mind if we have lunch together before we talk?" she asked.

George was still numb with fear and could not say anything. He just nodded and the policeman sat down.

She talked nonstop during lunch, but George was still ill at ease with the presence of the policeman and said very little. Luckily, immediately after he finished eating, the policeman excused himself saying that he had to catch the bus back home and left them.

After the waitress had cleared their plates, she turned to him, the smile gone from her face and asked sternly, "If we are going to work together, I need to know the whole truth, and nothing but the truth. You stole this cheque, didn't you?" It was a statement, not a question.

George kept quiet for some time. He knew very little about this woman. Apart from her name, which he had read from the name tag she wore, he did not know anything else about her. Was it safe to trust her? On the other hand, did he have an option. He was already committed to her by giving her the stolen cheque. He glanced at her, and found her studying him closely. Her eyes were no longer smiling. George wondered what she was thinking about.

Lucy was noting the different expressions playing on George's face. She could see the hesitation in his eyes. But she had expected that. After he had given her the cheque, she had rushed and gone to see her boss. He had given her the green light to take the risk and initiate him into the club.

What George did not know was that they had already made a thorough check on him and decided that he was good enough for the club. With an uncle working for a powerful corporation as the chief accountant, and given his own naivety, he was going to be a useful asset for the club.

But they had not also overlooked the fact that George was as smart as he was naive. He had already proved himself. One, by having escaped from the confines of village life to come to the city, two, by deciding to hand over the briefcase containing money, and going for the less obvious stealing the cheque instead. Nor could they miss the fact that the boy had a burning ambition. But above all, he was trusted by his bosses, at least enough to entrust him with cheques and cash to deposit on the corporation's account.

The policeman bit had been a bluff. Lucy had no brother who was a policeman; actually the 'policeman' had been Daniel, one of the members of the club. But it had had its effect. She had seen how frightened he had been. Yes, tough little thieves like him had to be dealt with toughly. Just to remind him that if he 'misbehaved', she could always call upon her policeman brother.

"Yes, I stole it," George finally answered.

"Thought so," Lucy replied. Her mind coming back to the present. "But that is not the point. The point here is that this is a very fat cheque, though that is incosequential too because it can be made even fatter and the names of the payee can also be altered..." She was talking so softly that George had to strain to catch what she was saying.

"How?" George whispered back.

"All you need is an account number," she continued in the same quiet tone.

"How do I get one?" George could not hide his excitement.

"I'm going to have to initiate you into the network. You have to meet the boss, but first things first. Come, we can't talk here."

She led him outside the restaurant into the parked car. She slid into the drivers seat and George sat in front with her.

"What... Where are we going," George asked, alarmed, as the car sped away from the restaurant.

She did not answer. Soon, she came to a stop in front of a big building, in one of the outskirts of the city. "Come," she said to him and George followed her inside.

They entered a dingy looking room which was faintly lit. There seemed to be no sign of anyone. George hesitated, not wanting to proceed. But Lucy produced a tiny remote control and pressed a few keys. The door immediately opened, slowly and quietly. She beckoned to him to follow her. There was a group of about six men working on the table with papers, scissors, stamps and a strange-smelling ink. She led him past the men, into an inner room and invited him to sit down. There was another person in the room, hidden by the dirty curtain partitioning the small room from the 'workshop'.

"This is George Walusimbi," Lucy announced to the man seated in the shadows. "He is ready to join the club."

The man nodded and said nothing.

"Right now, I'm going to tell you only the basics." Lucy began. "You will pick the rest as you get more involved."

George nodded, not knowing what to say.

"We are involved in a very risky, but interesting and profitable business, that is if you follow the rules. We obtain cheques, traveller's cheques, credit cards and bank drafts through many ways. We clean them, and alter a few things before cashing them for money."

George had no idea what she was talking about, but he did not say so.

Lucy went on to explain how their operation worked. Members of the club obtained cashed traveller's cheques from the banks in the neighbouring countries, including South Africa , with all the stamps and signatures. Then they would be cleaned with special rubbers and ink and put back into circulation. Alternatively, they bought new ones of a lower denomination, say of $10 or $20 and added several zeros.

Others worked with people in the post office and intercepted the cashed traveller's cheques before they reached their destination. Apart from traveller's cheques, cheques were also stolen from both banks and the post office. The same process of cleaning would be followed and names of payees and figures altered.

"Each one of us has a role to play," Lucy continued. "From today, you will be assigned a role. Of course I don't have to emphasise the need for secrecy and trust in this business. We take vows, committing ourselves never to give away each other. But in case, due to unforeseen circumstances , you divulge the names of the people you work with, then your own neck will be at stake too because of the role you play. So we are in this together, it is teamwork. Do you have any questions?"

George was momentarily puzzled. Why did they assume that he wanted to join their club. A club of thieves. On the other hand, what was going to happen to the cheque he had surrendered to Lucy?

"What about my cheque?" he blurted out.

"It has already been taken care of," Lucy answered impatiently. "You will receive a substantial amount of money for your involvement, that is for having obtained it. But as I have explained, this is teamwork and each one of the players has to be paid for their services."

Well, George thought, what else was there left for him to say? He had always wanted to make money, and here was the chance to do it!

"I will try it out," he said at length.

"That is not good enough," Lucy snapped. "We need your total commitment. Here," she got the piece of paper which the man who had been sitting in the shadows held out to her, and handed it to George. "These are the rules. Read through them and when you are ready, you can come back here and sign. He will be the witness," she said, pointing to the man in the shadows.

"And about your money," Lucy continued, "come to the bank tomorrow and I will help you open a checking account where we shall deposit it." She got up to leave. George sat without moving, still holding the set of rules she had given him. "If you want a lift, I can drive you back to the city," Lucy added, her trademark smile returning. It was impossible to believe that she was the tough-talking woman George had just been listening to.

"Thanks," George said standing up. He was not going to let this woman think that she had a hold on him- already.

They are already treating me like a prisoner, and they are making too many assumptions, George thought as they drove back to the city centre. He did not like the way it smelt.

"Right. See you tomorrow," Lucy said as he got out of the car. He did not answer. He was going to think very seriously about the whole thing. He hadn't understood much of what she had said but what he knew was that they were a bunch of smart thieves. And, it seemed they knew how to make money. Well, he was not going to jump into their wagon, not yet. He would ask someone, a friend maybe, if they knew anything about this gang of thieves. And of course, he would see if they were going to honour their promise about the cheque he had given Lucy.

**

"He is okay," the man who had been sitting behind the shadows said. "He is ambitious and smart. And we need him. He has already stolen a cheque, and there could be more where that one came from."

A small meeting had convened immediately George had left. Lucy had just wanted to get rid of him, so that she could get the opinion of her boss. Soon after dropping him in the city, she had come back to the dingy room. There had been two other people sitting behind the closed door, listening to the conversation between Lucy and George.

What George did not know was that he was being tailed. From that time, until he accepted to sign, they would not let him out of their sight. And what Lucy had not told him was that the network involved state security agencies such as the police. And if George made the stupid decision to go to the police or worse still, failed to turn up at the agreed time, then his body would be found in a ditch somewhere, his unfortunate death attributed to mugging.

The following day, George was among the first 'customers' to stand in the queue at Lucy's counter.

She smiled at him and beckoned him to go behind. She had all the forms needed to open a checquing account. Within a short time, he had a checquing account number. When George looked at the amount on his newly opened account, his mouth went dry at the sight of so much money. Lucy was watching him and she saw the desired effect. Now, he would not hesitate to sign the set of rules earlier given to him, she thought, satisfied.

Chapter Three

Somehow, George managed to contain his euphoria and carry on his duties both at home and at the office normally. He only allowed himself to dream and smile at night in the privacy of his room. What would he do with all that money, he often wondered to himself. If he bought a car, or built a house, everyone would be suspicious of him. Yet he did not want to squander it on booze and good clothes. What would he invest in.

He thought of buying fishing nets and boats, and investing in the fishing business, but he found the idea of going back to the island repulsive. Besides, that business was for small-time people, not for a 'millionaire' like him.

At the corporation, he had now turned into a hero. People admired him for his candour. Even his uncle was proud of him. After all, how many people were 'daft' enough to hand over a briefcase full of money to the police. He now entrusted to him the duty to clean and dust his office, something he had never allowed anyone to do before. He was suspicious of everyone and never wanted his paperwork to be tampered with. And of course, he had to be careful with the cheques he kept locked in his drawers.

***

As he got more and more involved in the club's dealings, George came to learn that it was a very risky business. No one trusted the other, and you had to be constantly on your toes, otherwise you'd be robbed blind. George's immediate task had been to obtain other cheques, (the word 'steal' was never used in their club) from the corporation. But he was finding it very difficult to fulfill his first assignment.

His uncle kept all the cheque books under lock and key. He could not steal the ones he was given to deposit on the corporation's account; that would be very stupid of him. He decided to take his time and instead learn more about how the network worked. He continued to do small-time jobs like delivering messages and getting more contacts for the network. For this, he was paid a small fee.

He learnt that one could easily 'buy' already cashed cheques, worth a lot of money, from the banks. All you had to do was to get acquainted with the person responsible for disposing of cashed cheques and traveller's cheques. This way, he could remove at least five (making sure that they were drawn on large corporations which would not easily miss the money) and sell them to you for a small fee, before burning the rest of the used cheques.

The rest was easy. The cleaning process would start, erasing the 'paid' stamps, names of payee, and amount. The cheques would then be taken to an expert on signature writing, and the cheque would be as good as new, ready to be re-cashed. But the ones stolen from the post office were the easiest to deal with because they were already 'clean'.

Credit cards were also easy to steal, especially from the tourists. These would be used to buy goods anywhere credit was given.

One other thing George learnt was that cheques and traveller's cheques were not always used to obtain cash. Most were sent to suppliers abroad of mostly, consumable goods. By the time the company from which the cheque had been stolen got a bank statement from their bankers, showing that an unknown cheque had been cashed on their account, the transaction would already have taken place.

Of course the banks always tried to trace the person who had deposited the cheque, but without success. The companies used to receive the goods were registered in false names; and in most cases, were nonexistent. These 'free' goods were used to open large shopping malls in the city.

George had also managed to obtain such goods after he had bought a used cheque, and he had opened a small shop on Luwum Street, one of the busiest streets in the city. From the shop, which he had put in charge of a worker, and from the little money he made from the odd jobs he did for the club, he was slowly beginning to make some meaningful savings. Then there was the windfall which he had made from the stolen cheque. This, he kept on his account until he plotted what to do with it.

The corporation had tried to question him if he had already handed over the cheque by the time the accident had happened, and he had answered in the affirmative.

But he needed to make real money. He wanted to build a mansion, like some members of the club had built, drive a sleek Mercedes Benz, and own beautiful mistresses. Whenever he tried to ask the older members how they managed to steal the cheques or credit cards without being caught, they would laugh in his face and say that he only had to jump at opportunities.

"But how do I know what is an opportunity and what isn't?" he had asked.

"You don't; you have to keep jumping."

They had also warned him that it was extremely risky. He needed no other evidence of this than the incident of two members of the club who had been nabbed from abroad after they were found in possession of counterfeit money. The two had appeared in court and were sentenced to five years imprisonment. Luckily, only close family members got to know because they were not prominent people in the government. But still, the club members were shaken and business slackened a bit.

***

Then one day, his second chance knocked. His uncle was taken ill for one week, and when he recovered, his doctor told him to take some more days off and have a good rest because he had signs of developing high blood pressure. But he was not the kind to stay at home just resting. He asked his nephew to go to his office and bring him some files so that he could work at home. George immediately knew that this was an opportunity, and he had to 'jump'.

He ransacked through the drawers of his uncle's office, but he did not find what he was looking for. His uncle had carefully removed the keys to the two drawers where George suspected the cheque books were locked before giving him the bunch of keys to his office.

He was about to lock the office when an envelope, lying on top of the neatly kept files in one of the drawers, caught his attention. It was so similar to the one he had been given to deliver to the now deceased businessman in Masaka. His heart leapt. He quickly opened it, and indeed, inside, was a cheque, duly signed, and stamped. He had no idea how he left the office, his heart pounding with excitement.

In the quiet of his miserable room, where he still slept at his uncle's house, he sat and planned. He had no intention of letting the others know about this stolen cheque, not even Lucy. This time, he was not going to share his loot with anyone save for the boys who did the cleaning, and the one who wrote the signatures. And even then, he would pay them only a token. He was sure that they too wanted to make an extra shilling by doing a side job which their bosses did not know about.

He had gathered enough information about the banking system and how it operated. He knew what it took to open a checking account. There were several banks which had recently sprung up in the city. These banks were more preoccupied with getting as many clients as possible, rather than getting to know who their clients were. No referees were required to recommend one to open an account and very little attention was paid to the client while withdrawing money.

He went to work, patiently. First, he had to work on his identity, grow a beard and shave his head clean. He also 'developed' an eye problem and was 'recommended' by an eye specialist to start wearing spectacles.

The secretaries at the office teased him mercilessly that he wanted to look academic with spectacles to impress them. But that they were not interested and advised him to try the teagirls. They said the beard made him look like a Moslem Tabliq.

He was not bothered by any of it; if anything, his new identity was proving to be more authentic than he had thought.

Patience and more patience was the word if he wanted to do a neat, untraceable job.

***

It took Ntambi sometime to realise that a thief had broken into his office and stolen a company cheque. But when he did, he did not panic. First, it was going to be easy to catch the thief, it was a matter of alerting the banks and the thief would be caught trying to deposit it. Secondly, the cheque was worth very small money, just fifty thousand shillings, which the corporation could afford to lose in case the thief was not in position to refund it.

But still, it was bad enough that a thief had had access to his office, and there could be a repeat of it. Being the thorough man that he was, he combed through all the avenues he thought the thief might have used to break into his office. He went through the list of people who had entered his office in the recent past, but found none whom he could be suspicious of. But as a measure of protection, he stopped entrusting his office keys to his nephew lest a thief took advantage of the boy's naivety to steal more cheques.

***

George waited for six months before opening the account. He used false names, which accompanied his newly acquired identity of a bespectacled, slightly bearded young man who could pass as a diploma student in an up country college. He had been waiting for signs from his uncle which would show that he was suspicious of him, or for him to mention what steps he was taking to catch the thief, but none came. So he went ahead and executed his plan. He knew he had to wait for four working days to elapse before the cheque could mature into cash.

The waiting was hell; he was so impatient to know if he had managed to pull off his first job. Yet when the fourth day finally arrived, he felt apprehensive about going to the bank to check.

He managed to gather enough courage and went to the bank. Soon, he was standing in front of the teller. He filled in the small paper, making a formal request to know the balance on his account. The teller scanned the paper professionally and pressed some keys on the computer. George saw a shadow fall on her face and her forehead crease. She pressed more keys and waited as more figures jumped on the screen. Still, she did not seem satisfied. She got off the high stool and went to the back. George looked around him wildly. Two guards were stationed at either side of the entrance and seemed to be waiting for him to make a move so that they could arrest him. She was gone for a very long time.

"Sorry for the delay," the teller had come back and was talking to him, "but I think there is a small problem with your account. If you will come with me, I will take you to the manager."

Alarm bells began to ring in his head. "Ah...I don't think...I have the ti...time," he was stammering terribly. "Mayyy...be..."

"This won't take long, please follow me," the teller insisted.

He could not run now, the guards would arrest him. Besides, it might not be serious at all. He followed the teller to one of the offices behind the counters. She held the door for him and invited him to enter. George entered and stopped dead.

He gazed at Lucy, seated there, with another woman and he broke into a cold sweat. He began to tremble. All he could think about was how Lucy had found out about him. She was watching him and her face

100

was expressionless.

"Sit down," the other woman in the office told him. He slumped into the chair opposite Lucy's, gratefully. At least now he wouldn't collapse, he thought.

Lucy was still watching him, her eyes becoming mere slits. He wished she could say something.

"How did you find out about me," George whispered, unable to bear the silence and Lucy's piercing eyes.

"You are actually very stupid, aren't you," Lucy said, standing up. "Did you, in your small mind, imagine that you'd pull off this? Alone? You must have imagined you were the smartest thief to walk this earth! Or did you imagine that there was a bank in this country stupid enough to honour a one hundred million shilling cheque without making some inquiries from the company where it was being drawn from or that pathetic 'identity switch' would convince anyone except yourself? Bastard!" She spat out and George jumped.

"Mr Walusimbi," the other lady addressed him, "we are not here to quarrel. Lucy is a bit upset. We are here to tell you the options open to you. Remember, we work as a team. It is a network and we have members in all the major banks. So there was no way you could have pulled off this without us knowing."

What is she trying to explain to me, George thought, confused. The shock of being discovered was still clouding his thinking and he was not following what they were talking about.

"Are you going to hand me over to the police," he asked in a trembling voice.

"Of course not. You see, we are not as dumb as you are. We happen to have brains in our heads, you know, not porridge, as in your case," Lucy said, enjoying every moment of it.

"I think you know the rules of the club, Mr Walusimbi," the other lady said, now speaking calmly. "You know what happens when one member tries to defect, or when that member puts the necks of the other members in danger, just like you did. You were going to be arrested; they'd only wait for the person who opened the account in those names to appear, inquiring about the fat cheque he had deposited. And before anyone knew it, you'd be singing like a parrot - singing the names of the others you work with.

"Of course we could not let that happen, so we intercepted the cheque before the bosses got hold of it. We shall go ahead and cash the cheque, and as the rules say, each member who has played a role will be paid for their services."

"Now get out," Lucy shouted. "Come to the bank tomorrow for your share."

George slowly got to his feet. All energy seemed to have drained out of him. He did not know whether to laugh or cry. Somehow, he managed to reach the door and he let himself out.

"You scared the shit out of him, didn't you," the other lady said to Lucy, suppressing a smile.

"That will teach him a good lesson," Lucy answered. "But you cannot write off the boy as completely daft; at least he chose the 'right' bank to come to."

George did not bother to go to the bank where Lucy worked the following day. He did not want to see her smug face after the way she had treated him the previous day. Besides, he knew she would never honour her promise; he had messed this one up and he had himself to blame.

Chapter Four

When Ntambi received the bank statement for that month, he was left agape at the amount missing from the corporation's account which he presumed had been stolen using the stolen cheque.

Real fear gripped him when he realised what the implications would be. He would be suspect number one of course. He could even be interdicted. His integrity as a meticulous, trustworthy, and experienced accountant shattered. He had to tell the managing director right away.

The managing director was sympathetic but shocked, nonetheless and immediately suggested calling in the Criminal Investigation Department. He also decided to call an impromptu board of directors' meeting to inform them about the shocking news.

All these decisions did not calm Ntambi's fears. He knew what it would mean if the information leaked to the nosy press. He requested the managing director to give him more time so that he could make investigations on his own and bring the thief to book, but the latter refused.

"Mr Ntambi, these are company funds we are talking about; we cannot keep quiet any more," he told him. "Besides, you know very well what the corporation has just been through; I don't want to fall victim to the scandals which befell the former MD."

The corporation had been thrown into disarray when the former MD was sent on forced leave and many top dogs suspended because of mismanagement of funds. The corporation already had a bad image and could not afford any more scandals.

Before they could start on any work, the CID recommended that Ntambi be suspended so that he could not interfere with their investigations or use his office to block evidence.

Ntambi was suspended for six months on charges of misuse of office and neglect of his duties which led to the corporation's loss of a colossal amount of money.

Ntambi's name was splashed all over the front pages of newspapers. *The Monitor,* an independent daily went as far as saying that Ntambi had stage-managed the smartest theft of the year.

He was devastated. He knew his career as a reputable accountant was finished. Just because of one lousy thief, his name was tarnished forever. All his life's hard work had been flushed down the toilet.

George was also interrogated by the CID and asked to give a statement. His uncle had disclosed that he was the only person he had ever entrusted with his office key. Everyone at the corporation, however, vouched for George's integrity as the most trusted messenger the corporation had ever employed. Out of routine, however, an impromptu search of George's quarters was mounted, bu. no money, or anything related to the stolen cheque was found.

***

Things were happening too fast for George to comprehend. The CID were working very fast. He had heard his uncle say that they had finally located the bank in which the cheque was deposited and they were trying to find the person who deposited it!

He had never heard from Lucy again, but after the grilling interrogation from the CID, and the scaring news from his uncle, he felt like talking to someone from the club who would advice him and give him some assurance. So he went to see Lucy.

She did not seem surprised to see him. George told her about the news from his uncle, but she did not seem bothered. Instead she asked him if he had come to collect his share from the stolen cheque!

"How can you talk of money when we are in this shit!" George burst out. He was getting irritated by her callousness.

"Do you want it or don't you?" Lucy asked calmly.

He looked at her for a long time. "I want it," he said finally, making up his mind. He had long come to the decision to quit the club. Having been beaten at his own game, he knew that he would never be able to operate without the others. And this meant that he would never be able to make real money on his own. Besides, he was shaken by the events following the cheque he had stolen. It was too dangerous a game to play. He had even decided not to get his share of it, but now he had changed his mind. If he was to quit, he would rather leave rich.

"I will put it on your account," Lucy said in a dismissive tone.

George left without saying another word.

***

The forced leave was beginning to take its toll on Ntambi. His shoulders were stooped and his eyes sunken. He rarely spoke. He had also developed a short temper, and he often snapped at his wife and kids, something George had never known him to do. As the days passed into weeks, and the CID were not through with their final report yet, Ntambi sank deeper into depression. He never left his house and refused to answer the door or any calls. The only people he talked to were the CID and only because it was required of him to keep furnishing them with information.

His wife tried to console him. "I believe you are innocent, and that's all that matters; what other people and the press say does not matter."

"Who could it be?" he kept on asking himself. He questioned George again and again, whether he remembered seeing anyone enter his office, or if by mistake he had forgotten the keys in the door after cleaning, but George insisted that he had been careful with the keys.

Ntambi refused to eat and as a result became frail. He spent more time in bed thinking and contemplating. His mind kept going back to George. If he swore that he never left the keys out of his sight, then he was the only person who could have had the chance to look at that missing cheque. But the CID had cleared him; besides, George would not know what to do with the cheque. As far as he knew, the boy was illiterate and green.

The high blood pressure, which he had developed earlier that year, came back with a vengeance, this time coupled with stomach ulcers.

"The only cure for you is to stop overloading your brain with so much worry. Get out of bed, eat your meals regularly, and get some exercise," the doctor told him.

He tried hard not to think of his nephew as the smart thief who had managed to walk away with a cool one hundred million shillings, but the nagging feeling at the back of his head would not go away. He thought of confronting him with the knowledge that he actually knew

105

who the thief was, but that was unwise because George could decide to bolt and then he would be in hot soup again.

He thought of telling the CID about his suspicions regarding George, but would they believe him? They would want to know why he had not told them before, and matters would be worse if it was discovered that he was his 'godfather' at the corporation.

A week went by, and still Ntambi could not bring himself to confront his nephew. His high blood pressure was getting worse. He woke up one night to find his whole body drenched in sweat. His heart was pounding fast and his lower body felt paralysed and cold. He tried to move his arms but they, too, were like loads of stone, and could not move. He opened his mouth to call his wife but no sound came out of it.

Sweet Jesus, what is happening to me, Ntambi thought in panic. He could see his wife shaking him vigorously and faintly hear her calling his name but he could not respond. As he lay there, immobile, his vision began to blur and he felt as if a heavy object was pressing down his heart, making it increasingly difficult for him to breathe. He felt extremely tired and closed his eyes to try and sleep. But the pressure on his heart was increasing and breathing was now impossible. He felt himself falling down...down...into the deepest slumber ever.

When his wife finally got him to hospital, the doctor informed her that Ntambi had suffered a massive cadiovascular arrest which is always fatal.

***

The events following Ntambi's death were as shocking as his untimely death. The CID had managed to locate the bank where the stolen cheque had been deposited, and later, the one hundred million shillings drawn. They had also established the identity, at least according to the false ID, names and picture on the file, of the person who had deposited it.

It was also obvious that the thief had not worked alone, definitely there had been some internal collaboration and they were determined to find it.

Two days later, however, the screaming headlines in the newspapers jolted, not only the CID, but the entire public to their roots. The bank where the stolen cheque had been deposited, together with several others, had been indefinitely closed by the Central Bank after

106

they had been declared insolvent.

There were pictures of stranded clients standing outside the banks' premises, wondering what would happen to their deposits. Businesses came to a halt as people could not get access to cash. The Central bank promised to issue a statement soon, to clarify on reasons for the bank's closure and what the fate of the depositors would be. The directors of the closed banks were reported to be in hiding and others had even fled the country. For the moment, there was nothing the CID could do. They only had to wait until the banks re-opened.

In the meantime, the thief, or thieves could easily walk away with their loot and there was nobody who could stop them because with the banks closed, the CID could not obtain any incriminating evidence.

Chapter Five

George waited for six months after the death of his uncle and closure of the banks before he made his first move. To his astonishment, Lucy had kept her promise and deposited his share from the stolen cheque on his account. And by God, what a share! He had walked away with the lions share. He was rich...rich...rich.

Later, when Lucy accepted his resignation from the club, he was even more surprised. He had not expected them to let him off the hook so easily, given his ample knowledge about the network. Probably they were shaken by the closure of all the banks where they had had contacts.

It was now time to show those fancy secretaries at the office, who treated him like some sort of trash, that he could own them all if he wanted to.

What the hell do you think you are. I could buy every goddamn person in this office and still be rich, he thought furiously. The six months seemed like years, but it was important to let the storm abate.

He began by buying a second-hand nine-seater commuter bus. This, nonetheless, raised many eyebrows.

"Do you think he had a hand in that missing cheque?" some were heard speculating.

"I don't think so, the boy is as green as fresh vegetables when it comes to matters concerning money. Remember when he handed over that briefcase full of money to the police."

"But of course he couldn't, the boy is so honest that he even brings back a balance of one hundred shillings."

"Don't you know that his uncle left him some money when he died? He loved his nephew so much. Besides, George has been saving every shilling he earns now for the last five years."

So many things were said but nothing came of it. Meanwhile, the commuter taxi was bringing in a reasonable amount of money and it, therefore, came as no surprise when George quit his low-paying job to concentrate on his business. After that, no one paid much attention to him. Sometimes he drove the taxi himself, but most of the time he was busy hatching a plan to utilise his accumulated wealth.

A few months later, he sold the second-hand taxi and bought a brand-new fourteen seater. Then he began putting up small structures in the slum areas of the city and made one of them his temporary home. He was careful to keep a low profile and, to the outside world, he was simply another serious, hardworking, but determined young man who was slowly but steadily rising to the top.

George had completely lost contact with his late uncle's family. After the burial of Ntambi, George's father and his aunts had openly accused the late Ntambi's wife of having had a hand in the death of their brother.

"She wanted to take all the property," one of Ntambi's sisters said. "You see, her own family is so poor and she has been building them a brick house, I hear."

"It seems she had got herself another lover and wanted her husband out of the way. You can even see that the last born is not Ntambi's child. She is too brown to belong to our clan. And those ears! As large as those of a rabbit! Our ancestors never had such ears," the head of the clan contended.

They refused to believe the 'fabricated story that Ntambi had sometime before his death developed high blood pressure. At a meeting which was convened the day after the heir, who was Ntambi's eldest son, was installed, it was decided that the widow should leave the kids with George's father on the island, and go back to the city, sell the house and other property, then bring everything else to the island where their rightful owner, the heir, would be living thereafter. Then she would be free to go and pursue her own plans.

The widow pretended to go ahead with their suggestions, too disgusted to argue with these illiterate relatives of her late husband. She told them that she would have to take the kids back to the city to complete their third term and get their reports; then she would do as they had requested.

When she went back to the city, she sold the house and the car plus the other property, then flew to London with all her kids to live with her sister. Before she left, she gave George her new address and begged him to write to them.

"You can even come and visit us one day," she told him. "I don't want my children to forget their late father's people."

***

George loved beautiful things; but beautiful things did not come cheap: they were bought with lots of money. But neither was he a pauper. From the careful investments he had made, he had become one of the 'millionaires' in the city, at least in the eyes of his former colleagues in the club. And it was high time he began living like one. Besides, everybody could vouch for his 'undisputed' rise to the top in the last two years.

He began by building a house, and when it was completed, George could not help but feel like a real millionaire. The six bed-roomed mammoth of a house, built in the exclusively -for-the-rich residential area of Ntinda was expensively and lavishly furnished. He had hired an equally expensive interior designer who had seen to it that no expenses were spared in trying to give George his money's worth.

Indeed, the grandeur of the mansion was evidence that Lisa, the interior designer, had kept her part of the promise. The exquisite furniture had been ordered from 'Kazinga Channel', the best furniture suppliers in town. The two-inch thick wall-to-wall carpets were from South-East Asia while the curtains were done in soft but rich multicoloured fabrics which looked extremely gorgeous. The original oil paintings, the gold-rimmed wall clock and glass coffee tables were absolutely stunning.

The only thing George missed was the water. He had grown up surrounded by it; and he sort of missed its cooling effect and the sound of waves as they splashed on the wet and slippery rocks.

George hated pets: they made his skin crawl, but Lisa had confided in him that it was fashionable to keep them. So he obtained a Persian cat which he named Pepe. After two months, Pepe had grown quite big. What George hated most about Pepe was it's complacent nature. Whenever he looked at it, sleeping peacefully in his sofa, he felt like strangling it. The stupid cat would never know how hard he had worked to attain such comfortable furniture. It was content to lie in deep slumber for the whole day and not give a damn about anything in the world! Not even about what it would eat. The stupid fool, why couldn't pets be a little more ambitious like other animals!

Lisa had also introduced him to the right choice of clothes, shoes and perfumes. He owned more suits than he could possibly need. Leather

110

belts with golden buckles, Clarks shoes, which had cost him a fortune, filled his wardrobes. Lisa also helped him choose the right and latest CDs which he played on his expensive Akai music system.

She also went a step further and introduced him to the Rotary Club, an association of the rich and professionals, as her guest. His classification was 'Export and Import services'. George often wondered exactly what that meant. But he never dwelt much on it; what he knew was that he had been accepted in a class of the elite and rich people who made important decisions which affected people's lives. In short, people who mattered. What more could he ask for than the chance to rub shoulders with people like the Chief Judge of Uganda, or newspapers moguls, not to mention ministers and other powerful politicians!

These 'powerful' connections however did not come without a price. In order to maintain a meaningful conversation with these people, he had to keep abreast with current world events which meant that he had to listen to the BBC, and read numerous newspapers. He also had to learn to play different kinds of sports like golf which many of those Rotarians played.

Deep inside, he loathed it all; the energy it took to try and fit in, to belong. He hated the Friday evening fellowships when he could have been at *Hakuna Matata* joint enjoying roast pork with his other less important friends whom he felt more comfortable with. He did not mind dishing out money for their numerous projects like Polio-Plus, meant to help the less fortunate people in society, but what he hated was being kept on his toes trying to participate in their 'complex' conversation.

He remembered the incident at the dinner party to install the club's President when he had suddenly found himself caught in the middle of a conversation with some big shots in town.

"Ah...Mr Walusimbi," one of them had started, "forgive my short memory, but I think we were together at Makerere University, except I can't remember your hall of residence. Northcote, was it?"

"He certainly looks like a Northcoter," another one joined in and they laughed heartily.

George smiled stiffly and replied, "No."

"Oh then it must have been Livingstone, and I think we were in the same year. Oh, you must be thinking I'm feigning ignorance, but these days we do load our minds with so much that we can even forget the names of our wives, don't we?" The other people around burst out in laughter, but George did not laugh.

He felt like hitting the man's smug face. There was a twist of laughter at the corners of his mouth and George knew that he must have intended to embarrass him.

I have never been to any fucking university, George almost screamed in anger. Yet I have as much as you have, even more. Yes, even that elegant, fancy Lisa, I'm bedding her, do you hear? And didn't she tell me that she was at the University of Iowa, in the USA, where she studied architecture!

But he did not say all these aloud; he managed to contain his anger and kept on smiling stiffly till the men walked away.

He was seething with anger by the time the party ended. After that incident, he decided to quit the Rotary Club. He was tired of being looked down upon, as if he was a nobody. Even that motto of theirs was sickening: 'Service Above Self', it said. No man in his right senses should believe in that ridiculous motto.

Lisa was mad at him. "You can't just quit Rotary, you know. You must give a plausible reason," she tried to reason with him.

George did not want to hurt her, especially after all that she had done for him. But what about what he had done for her? George thought. Hadn't he paid her back? Sometimes when he thought of all the money he had spent on her, he shuddered. Those gold necklaces and earrings she insisted on buying from the USA or South Africa because the ones in Uganda were apparently mere imitations! And that piece of land he had recently bought for her in Kisaasi, a fast-growing suburb, where all the rich were rushing to acquire pieces of land. And boy, was it expensive! He could not imagine why she had refused to move in with him. His house was surely good enough for her tastes. But she was adamant, she wanted to live alone and be independent.

Meanwhile, he had to pay for the expensive apartment she was living in. Well, he wasn't complaining. After all, he could afford it. Actually he felt gratified that he could maintain such a sophisticated woman as Lisa. He always swelled with pride when they walked into a restaurant and he saw men's heads turn in admiration. Yes, beautiful women were everything: difficult to come by and maintain - like all the other beautiful things, but once you had them, you had to fight to keep them. One of these days, he was going to press her into marriage - seriously. He was so possessive of her. He wanted her for himself; he wanted to own her.

But for the Rotary, he had made up his mind: he was not going back there!

Chapter Six

George celebrated his twenty-fifth birthday with pomp and glamour. It was the first birthday he had ever celebrated in his lifetime and he felt awkward about it. But Lisa had insisted, saying that it was fashionable to celebrate birthdays these days. Now that he had acquired such a high status in society, it would be a shame if he ignored his birthday. And so he threw a lavish party. Most of the invited guests were Lisa's friends and she had arranged everything from the cake to the music, eats and drinks. There were loud cheers as he cut the three-tiered cake and blew the twenty five candles. He became even more uneasy as he mingled with the guests and sometimes forgot what to answer when they wished him happy birthday. How he wished Lisa could come to his rescue. But for the whole evening, he had not seen her. He wondered where she could have gone. Maybe she was out in the gardens with her female friends gossiping.

He was relieved when the last guest left. He was exhausted from the events of the evening and his face felt creased from the smile he had had to wear all evening for the sake of the guests. All he wanted to do now was find Lisa and go to bed. Yes, maybe a good screw would ease the tension in his muscles.

Thinking of sex, he felt his manhood harden and he hurried to go and find Lisa. He checked in two bedrooms and the kitchen, then the bathroom, but did not find her. He thought that perhaps she was already in his bedroom waiting for him. He hoped that this would not be one of those days when she decided that she wanted to spend the night at her place because she wanted to be alone.

He had nearly reached his bedroom when he remembered that he had not seen Simon, the guard lock the main gate. He decided to go and remind him in case he had forgotten.

The door to Simon's quarters was unlocked. He opened it and entered. The room was dimly lit.

"Simon," he called out. But there was no response. "Simon", he called out a bit loudly now, but still there was no answer. He was about to turn away when he thought that he had heard a sound in the inner room. He stepped further in and opened the door on his left, which led to the tiny sitting room. The room was also dimly lit but was soon illuminated by the light filtering in from the security light outside.

Then he saw them. Two figures lying naked on the floor. On closer inspection, he realised that the figures were that of a woman and a man and they were engaged in hot passionate lovemaking. The two lovebirds were apparently unaware of an intruder who had discovered their love nest and continued unperturbed with their game.

George swore silently. How many times had he told Simon that he should get himself a proper wife instead of screwing around with all the housemaids in the neighbourhood. In any case, he was supposed to be outside guarding his property and not lying in the arms of a woman. Why couldn't he wait for the guests to depart before he embarked on his little game?

George decided to deal with Simon in the morning. Maybe it was time to replace him. He felt his desire for sex mounting and he knew he had to go and find Lisa. He began to close the door, then his eyes caught sight of a dress lying on the floor. It was the same dress he had bought Lisa for the party and it had cost him a fortune. He would know it anywhere because of its beautiful flowery design.

George stood still for a moment. What the hell did this mean. Was this supposed to be some kind of a rude joke, or was he imagining things?

The man on top of the woman began to move faster and to make animal-like sounds while the woman under him screamed and called on her lover to ride her even harder.

George stood very still. The woman's voice, oh God that silky voice could not belong to anyone else except Lisa.

He stood transfixed, shockwaves vibrating through his whole body. He felt nausea rise up his throat. He willed himself to move away, away from that sickening scene in front of him, but his legs could not move. They had become stiff and cold. He began to quiver in anger and humiliation, and felt tears of betrayal and rage cloud his eyes.

Lisa, oh God, Lisa was all he could think about. He did not even realise that the two lovebirds had registered his presence and Lisa was desperately trying to cover her naked body while the man endeavoured to pull on his trousers.

George was like a possessed person. He was vaguely aware that he was moving towards the two people whom he believed to be still engaged in sex, his only intention to stop them. A blinding rage to kill the man suddenly overwhelmed him. He picked up the small table in front of him and with all the strength he could muster, hurled it at the man. The man let out a screech of pain as his hands flew protectively to his injured head. George was not yet done. With lightning speed, he lunged at him, his hands going for his windpipe.

"No," Lisa screamed, her voice full of terror. She knew she had to stop George. She got hold of another small table and hit him squarely on the head. George cried out in pain before falling down in a heap.

***

Simon was talking to the driver of the sleek limousine parked at the opposite side of the gate.

"Nice machine, no?"

"Yeah," the driver answered without much interest.

"Say, man, why didn't you park inside the gate?" Simon asked the driver.

"Boss' idea; he doesn't want the car to be seen at such night parties."

"It must be very tough, I mean, being a driver to these big shots. They leave you to sit in the car for ages as they drink themselves silly," Simon mused.

The driver shrugged indifferently but did not say anything. Simon reckoned that he was not in the mood to talk and decided to leave him alone.

He was about to turn away when he heard voices behind him. He turned and saw two figures approaching the vehicle. He stepped aside, not wanting the boss to see him talking to his driver.

He managed to see, through the shadows from his hiding place, a man walk unsteadily to the parked car, leaning heavily on a woman for support. The man was also uttering sounds of pain. Simon looked more closely at the two figures, the woman looked like Lisa and...sure enough, it was Lisa!

Before he could say anything, the door of the car opened and the man slumped inside followed by Lisa. The door was banged shut and the car sped off in the direction of the city centre.

115

Simon stared at the speeding car in confusion, UR2...he only managed to glimpse the bright red registration number. So it was a government car!

Simon was momentarily baffled. What had happened to the man. Had he fallen or was he simply drunk. And even then, what was Lisa doing with him.

He rushed back to the house. It was strangely quiet. He called out to his master, but there was no response. He checked in all the bedrooms and still did not find him and...where was his master then. The light in his quarters attracted his attention. He hadn't been there the whole evening and yet...he rushed there.

Simon felt aghast at the sight which greeted him when he entered his sitting room. His master lay sprawled on the floor, and blood had coagulated on his forehead. Broken furniture was thrown everywhere.

"Master," he called out to him softly.

George opened one eye, then the other. Both were swollen beyond recognition. He tried to get up, but it seemed too much of an effort for him and he slumped back with a cry of pain. Simon was instantly at his side trying to help him to his feet.

"My head," George whispered," I cannot." He could not continue.

***

The aftermath of what had transpired on his birthday party had slowly worn off and was now replaced by an anger George had not known existed in him. His whole being was totally consumed with a wild, violent, murderous anger. It was the indignation of being betrayed, the passion of an injured ego. A sense of hopelessness enveloped him for despite the rancour he felt towards these offenders, he still could not punish them.

The only thing which kept him sane was the thought that all this was an ugly nightmare from which he would wake up. That fateful night often came back to him, fresh as if it had happened yesterday.

That night, he had called Lisa, after the doctor, whom Simon had insisted on calling, was through with him. But she had not answered.

That is when the anger had begun to build up in him. He wanted to kill that man, with his bare hands, for taking away what belonged to him - exclusively. But before that, he would humiliate him in public. And the thought of calling his lawyer to see about the possibilities of suing the man who had assaulted him in his own house had entered his head.

Then the lies had started. The lawyer had tried to get evidence from

116

the guests who had attended the party but they were all tight-lipped. Those who spoke swore that they had not seen the accused at the party. This did not surprise George because almost all the guests had been Lisa's friends. The driver of the accused also swore that he had never driven his boss to any party on the day in question. As for Lisa, she had never talked to George and he did not even know where she was.

George's lawyer had regretfully informed him that he could not continue with a case which had only two witnesses: George and his guard, Simon.

"By the time a good prosecutor is through with Simon, his story will sound false even to himself. It will be the accused's word against his, and who is going to believe a guard with no education?" the lawyer told George. "Given the circumstances of the case, and the status of the accused, I suggest that you drop the idea of going to court."

A man of such high standing! George kept on thinking bitterly. Why had such a man, who could afford to rent a room in any hotel in the city, chosen to make love to Lisa in his own home. Unless one believed the rumours which circulated around that these big men in government could not control themselves when it came to sex. This same man was known for doing it to a woman at the back of his car as the driver watched. And also that he was fond of going to *Ange Noir* discotheque to pick up university students who normally peddled their flesh there and ended up in their university rooms.

And what about Lisa? What had driven her to this man's arms? Surely it couldn't be love. What could Lisa have possibly seen in such an ugly man with his large lips and bald head?

Well, whatever it was that had driven these two 'lovebirds', George was determined to punish them. One of his friends had told him of a good lawyer 'who could win any case'.

"He is the best there is," his friend had told him. "That is if he accepts to represent you. You see, his clients are referred to him by close associates, or other people of high repute. They don't go knocking on his door."

George could not think of anyone who could recommend him to this lawyer. Two of his friends, whom he had known while he was still a Rotarian, tried to put in a kind word for him, but the reputed lawyer would not even give them an appointment.

"For him, it is not only money," George remembered his friend saying. "He wants to know the family of the client he is dealing with and stuff like that."

George had no family to talk of. Who would know about his peasant father. Maybe if his uncle was still alive... Then an idea struck him; he could pretend that he was late Ntambi's son, maybe that would work.

George finally got to meet Magezi, the reputed lawyer, by using his late uncle's name.

"Yes, I knew the late Ntambi very well, we were at the university together. He was a man of such upright morals! I never once believed that crap about stealing money," Mr Magezi told him after he had introduced himself. "But my son, do you truly know the man you want to take to court?" he had asked him in astonishment. "I wouldn't touch him if I were you. The man has the reputation of destroying those who as much as disagree with government policies. He is extremely influential. He could destroy all your businesses. He has the power. After all, you were not even married to this woman; you have no claim over her. But if you insist, then I will go ahead and file a case of assault."

George told Mr Magezi to go ahead and file the case. He was determined to punish the 'big' man.

The case did not get to be mentioned until three months later and even then, the accused did not once appear in court because he was reportedly out of the country on state duties. Lisa was also out of the country and no one seemed to know where she was or when she would be back.

George was surprised that the case was never mentioned in any of the newspapers, including the independent ones.

"I told you the man has great influence: no one wants to be in his bad books," Mr Magezi explained to him.

It was George who later suggested that Mr Magezi withdraws the case.

"I'm extremely sorry," Mr Magezi told him sympathetically. But George did not feel sorry for himself; he had already decided that he was going to punish the two offenders using the 'other available means'. He was a man who believed in justice.

When he went to pay Mr Magezi for his time, the latter refused to take the money. "I did it for my old friend. I would never take money from Ntambi's son," he said.

And that seemed to be the beginning of their friendship. george became one of the family. At times, he did feel uncomfortable whenever he was in the old man's company; he could not help but feel that he did not deserve the friendship of one of the most powerful lawyers in town.

Chapter Seven

It wasn't that he had never seen her before during the many times he had been to the Magezis' house. It was just that he had never noticed her before. She had never opened the front door for him or sat with him in the sitting room alone. Somehow, she was always in the background. If she served them tea, she would quickly take away the tray after they had finished and would never be seen in the sitting room again.

So when she opened the front door for him one day and later sat with him in the sitting room, because Mr and Mrs Magezi were not around, George was suddenly struck by her beauty. She was tall and elegant. She was even a head taller than him. She had big luminous eyes which gave her a look of innocence. She had a gorgeous figure too, George noted as he followed her inside the house. And when she spoke, she did so quietly and deliberately as if she was dictating notes to him. When she smiled, it was a shy, hidden smile, as if she was not sure whether to smile or not. Nonetheless, it lit up her face, emphasising the soft lines around her mouth.

George wanted to know more about this child-woman, for despite her voluptuous body, he knew she was a mere child of less than twenty years. He was not deceived by the composure and the sense of maturity that she exuded. He could easily tell that she was painfully shy and even as he talked to her, he noticed her discomfort.

He gave her a message to deliver to the Magezis and left.

The next day, he called Mr Magezi to find out if he had received the message.

"Yes, Marina gave me the message," Mr Magezi answered.

"Who?" George asked slightly confused.

"Marina," Mr Magezi answered.

"Ah yes, yes," George said, trying to cover up his embarrassment. How could he confess to Mr Magezi that until that day, he had not known the girl's name. Marina. So that was her name? He rolled it on his tongue and it tasted nice.

Suddenly, he wanted to know everything about her. How was she related to the Magezis? What did she do? What was her favourite food? He had to find out.

After the experience with Lisa, he had sworn not to get close to any other woman again. Whenever he needed sex, he bought it straight from the prostitutes. What was the use of spending money on ungrateful girlfriends when one could get one's money's worth from these ever-willing women, he often told himself.

Somehow, Marina did remind him of Lisa. The two had almost the same structure, the big eyes, and complexion. But where Lisa was sophisticated and out-going, Marina looked simple and reserved. But one thing stood out distinctly: they were both very beautiful women.

He began finding excuses to go to the Magezis house. Not that he needed any, the Magezis treated him like one of the family and he was welcome to visit their home any time he wanted. He later learnt that Marina was Mr Magezi's niece whom he had brought to stay with them some two years before. But beyond that, they did not offer any more information concerning her.

***

As George continued to go to the Magezis house for the numerous dinner parties he was invited to, Marina too began noticing particular things about him. She could not think of what had first drawn her to him. Was it the exemplary manners he always exhibited whenever he was in the company of women, or the way he always handled himself as a gentleman, with perfect table manners? Maybe it was something which nature had bestowed on him which had first attracted her to him, like the dimples which appeared on his cheeks when he smiled.

Marina found herself looking forward to his visits, although she could not bring herself to be left alone in the same room with him. Even when he eventually invited her to go out to dinner with him, she could not accept his invitation.

"I thought you liked him," Mrs Magezi remarked.

"I don't know, Aunt," Marina answered in confusion. "I don't feel comfortable in his company."

"You don't feel comfortable in anyone's company, Marina," she rebuked her mildly. "Look, Marina, you should stop judging every man by one man's wrong deed. You are young and beautiful, and the only way you are going to live your life is by putting the past behind you."

Marina was used to this kind of talk from her Aunt, as she normally referred to Mrs Magezi. But still she refused to go out with George.

The first time she agreed to go out with him was to watch a live performance by Koffi Olomide, a renowned Paris-based Zaïrian musician who was visiting Uganda at the time.

"It would be a shame if you missed this one," Mrs Magezi said persuasively. George had bought tickets for all of them but as it turned out, the Magezis were not able to go because of other commitments.

"Go ahead," Mr Magezi encouraged her. "We shouldn't all disappoint George. After all, those tickets must have cost him a fortune."

And so she went. George had behaved like the gentleman he always was, bringing her home immediately the show was over and thanking her profusely for having accepted his invitation. Later, Marina could not explain the slight tinge of disappointment she felt when George did not even attempt to 'do anything.'

After that 'ice-breaking,' Marina could be seen in George's company almost every weekend. But never once did Marina say anything that even slightly suggested that she was getting interested in him.

"Don't you even like him?" asked her Aunt worriedly.

"I don't know, Aunt, but as I told you before, I don't feel comfortable in his company."

"Oh come on now, Marina, you are being over-sensitive again. At least give the man a chance; I'm not suggesting anything, but at least get to know him."

"I go out with him, Aunt, isn't that enough," Marina was slightly irritated by her Aunt's insistence.

"All right," her Aunt said, backing down. "I was only trying to be helpful. Listen Marina," she added after a moment, "how are you going to know that people care about you if you don't let them get close to you? You don't need to lock all the doors, you know. Open up, let people in, and that is the only way you will be able to tell the bad guys from the good ones."

Marina looked up at her Aunt but said nothing.

"Not all men are bad, Marina, okay? I know how much you have been hurt, but all that is in the past. That is why you came here, remember? To try and start anew."

Marina nodded her head.

"Then do that, Marina. Lower your guard a little, and for heaven's sake, respond to peoples feelings for you. Not only to the men, but to all those who want to get close to you. Give a little of yourself to them."

Marina nodded again, this time with tears welling up in her eyes. Mrs Magezi's kindness always did that to her. She did not know how to respond and often ended up crying.

She remembered when she had first come to live with them. She had been uneasy, wondering how she was going to cope or how she was supposed to respond to their kindness and show her gratitude. She had also wondered about their own children. How would they take to another 'child' coming to their home. But she had been surprised to find the house devoid of children. After a time, she had asked them where their children were.

"We have a wonderful daughter but she does not live here with us," Mrs Magezi answered.

"Why, where does she live?"

"She lives outside the country," Mrs Magezi said. "She goes to school there," she added.

"Don't you have pictures of her?" Marina wanted to know.

"I do, when I'm not busy, I will show them to you," she said quickly.

Mr Magezi looked rather uneasy and Marina noted that it was his wife who did the answering. She glanced at him and there was sadness in his eyes. She wondered what had caused it. She felt pity for him and an impulse to comfort him. He was such a warm person and pure...no, maybe celibate was the right word. Come to think of it, she had never seen him in intimate contact with his wife. The two acted more like friends than husband and wife.

Then there was the question of confidentiality. Would she be able to confide in them and tell them about her slain family, about Matayo...about Rosaria...and how she felt about her? Or would she shut them out too?

The first few days were very difficult. She was constantly homesick, home being the orphanage. She missed Father Marcel, Stella Maris, everybody. Even Rosaria. Yes, she missed Rosaria too. But was it possible for one to miss someone one had never loved?

She had only one picture of her, the one Father Marcel had sent her through the Magezis when they went to pick her from Hoima. Rosaria, then was only three; now she was four.

One day, Mrs Magezi had caught her looking at Rosaria's picture. "You must go and see her," she said quietly.

"Who?" Marina asked trying to put away the picture.

"Your daughter. I can understand how you must have felt then. You were a child yourself, and that harrowing experience you went through...but Marina, you are older now, and more responsible. I know you will love your child if you saw her now."

"You think so? I'm so terribly afraid that...that...I will not love her still."

"No. You will. I'm sure she misses you as much as you miss her."

"All right," Marina answered, "I will go."

"Marina!" Mrs Magezi had to shake her to break into her train of thoughts. "Do you understand?"

"Yes, Aunt, I'm going to give George a chance and..."

"...stop living like an introvert," Mrs Magezi ended for her.

PART THREE

Chapter One

As a baby, Rosaria had been easy to manage. She drank her milk well and she slept through the night. By eleven months, she was walking and by her first birthday, she was able to say a few words.

"We don't have to say anything about whose child Rosaria is," Father Marcel had said to Sister Bernadette and Matayo when they were returning from the hospital that day.

"She is just another orphan we have got from Hoima..." Father Marcel continued. "This way, Marina will have a chance to start anew, without the burden of a bad past hovering over her."

Sister Bernadette had agreed, and so had Matayo. They both thought it was the best thing to do at the moment. When the time was ripe, Marina would come and claim Rosaria as her child.

Rosaria was pampered by everyone. The other orphans referred to her as 'our baby'. She participated in every activity at the parish in her little way; going to the well to fetch water with the tiniest saucepan, going to the fields with a very small hoe which had been made specially for her, and sweeping the dormitory. She enjoyed singing, and always sat with the choir during Mass.

Rosaria liked dressing in the big dresses and shoes of the older girls. Often, she would 'steal' them from the suitcases of the bigger girls, and before anyone knew it, she would have run off to church to attend Mass, looking more like a scarecrow.

"Rosaria, go back and dress properly. Why didn't your big sister dress you, anyway?" Sister Bernadette would reprimand her gently. Big sisters were the bigger girls assigned to the smaller children to look after them until they reached an age when they could look after themselves.

"Funkwenda," she would reply, meaning she doesn't want to.

She had learnt to speak in a laughable way. She always put the syllable 'fu' at the beginning of every word. By the age of three though, she was a chatter-box.

"She is so different from her mother," Father Marcel remarked one day to Sister Bernadette.

"Yes. She is, in so many ways," Sister Bernadette replied thoughtfully.

Rosaria was inquisitive too, questioning everything around her. Like why they lived the way they did, and who her parents were.

"They are not dead," Father Marcel explained to her over and over again. "They live very far away and one day they will come and take you away."

"I would like that very much," Rosaria said.

"But we all love you very much, and we would miss you if you went away."

Father Marcel did not know that Rosaria was determined to find her parents. One day, she threw the whole parish into panic when she disappeared for a whole day. A search was mounted and the bushes and forests searched. It was the herdsman who later found her, lying in the cowshed. She said that she had gone to look for her parents, so when she got tired, she went to the herdsman to ask him for some milk, but he wasn't there and so she decided to take a nap.

Every Sunday after Mass, Rosaria went with Father Marcel to his residence to take tea with him and 'talk' to him. She refused to take the porridge offered at the orphanage on Sundays because it was normally served late. Sometimes Father Marcel was busy, or simply too tired and would have wished to lie down and rest, but it was difficult to refuse Rosaria anything.

One Sunday, she asked him, "Father, why is your skin white and not as black as ours?"

"It's because I was not born here," Father Marcel explained patiently.

"Where were you born then?"

"Italy."

"Wow, Italy! Where is that?"

"It's in Europe."

Her face creased in deep thought. "Is it far from here?" she asked

"Yes, Rosaria, it's very far from here."

"Is it as far as going to the well or to Hoima?"

Father Marcel bit his lower lip to stop himself from laughing. "It would take you many days to reach there," he answered smiling

"Then why did you leave your home to come here?" she asked, surprised.

"I wanted to bring the word of God."

"I see." Rosaria nodded her small head in an important way to show that she had understood such complex reasoning.

"Rosaria, now I really have..." Father Marcel began to say but Rosaria cut him short.

"Father, how many children does God have?"

Father Marcel shook his head resignedly.

"You don't know?" she asked incredulously when he took his time replying.

"It's not that, Rosaria. I just have a lot of work to do and-"

"Okay, answer only that and I won't disturb you again. Pleeeease," she begged him.

"All right," Father Marcel sighed.

"How many?" she prompted him.

"Many, Rosaria. Very many."

"Like these?" Rosaria asked demonstrating by putting her fingers together to make ten.

"Many more than those. You see, we are all children of God," Father Marcel answered patiently.

"Is God a woman or a man then," she asked again

"Neither, God is a spirit, and..."

"A spirit! What is a spirit?"

"Look Rosaria, you promised..."

"Okay, okay, next time." she said and ran off to go and play with her friends."

Father Marcel sighed. Sometimes Rosaria was too much. Maybe it was time for her to attend the catechism lessons which Matayo taught now. She would learn all she wanted from there.

***

On Good Friday, Rosaria always wept. The sad story of how Jesus was crucified on the cross although he was a good man made her feel so sad that she could not prevent the tears rolling down her cheeks. But what still puzzled her was that Jesus had managed to outdo his enemies and rise from the dead. She never tired to hear of that wonderful story and as usual, Father Marcel was the victim of her questioning.

"Father, tell me again about the story of Jesus' resurrection. Who first found out that Jesus had risen?"

"Rosaria, I told you that story last Easter and-"

"I have forgotten Father," Rosaria answered indignantly.

"All right," Father Marcel said giving in. "This one time, promise?"

Rosaria nodded her head and waited.

"It was Mary Magdalene who first found out," he started

"And what happened then?"

"Early Sunday morning," Father Marcel began, speaking slowly so that Rosaria would not have to interrupt him, "when it was still dark, Mary Magdalene went to the tomb and saw that the stone had been rolled away from the entrance-"

"And that was Saturday?" Rosaria interrupted.

"Sunday, I said it was on Sunday. It seems you are not paying much attention, Rosaria," Father Marcel reprimanded her gently.

"I am, Father, but then if Jesus died on Friday, why didn't that woman-"

"Not woman, Rosaria, her name was Mary Magdalene," he corrected her.

"Okay, why didn't Mary Magdalene go to the tomb on Saturday, why wait for Sunday?"

"She was afraid of the Jews. You see, after Jesus was killed, all the people he had been staying with went into hiding. They feared that they would be killed too. Besides, the tomb was being guarded."

Rosaria seemed satisfied and Father Marcel asked her, "Can I continue?"

She nodded her head.

"Well, Mary Magdalene went running to Simon Peter and the other disciple whom Jesus loved and told them that they had taken the Lord from the tomb and she did not know where they had put him. Then..."

"Who was the other disciple whom Jesus loved?" she interrupted him again

"John," Father Marcel answered.

"And Jesus loved him very much?"

"Yes, Rosaria."

"More than the others?"

"No," Father Marcel laughed. "Jesus loves us all and asks us to do the same."

"I'm tired," Rosaria announced.

"Very well. Today is Easter day and you ought to be enjoying yourself, anyway," Father Marcel told her and she ran off to go and find her friends.

Father Marcel often marvelled at how intelligent Rosaria was. She was always a shade more brilliant than the other children her age. She reminded him of Matayo when he was still young. She also had that trace of stubbornness and strong will which Matayo had possessed. He remembered the story of the 'missing groom' and how, Rosaria, because of her intelligence, had saved the embarrassing situation.

A couple, who had lived at the parish for many years had decided to eventually get married in church.

"Father, I have decided to get married and be able to share in the meal of Jesus Christ. Eat his body and drink his blood," the man told Father Marcel.

"Have you solved your problems then?" Father Marcel asked happily.

"Yes, Father, I have decided to send away the other woman and remain with my youngest wife. I will provide for the other woman and her children."

"If that is your decision, then I have no objection."

A date for the wedding day was set and Rosaria, with two other orphans were chosen as bridesmaids.

Come the wedding day, Rosaria and the other brides- maids dressed in white dresses with matching hats. As they sat waiting for the bride to be ready, Rosaria got impatient and decided to go and show off her white attire to the groom and his people who were also getting ready in Matayo's house. Matayo was going to be the best man. But she was surprised not to find them there. She called out but the house was empty. Then she went behind the house, and there she saw the groom hurrying away, almost running to the further end of the banana plantation.

Rosaria immediately knew that something was amiss and began running after the groom, calling to him to come back. But the faster she ran, the faster the groom ran, putting more distance between them. Rosaria began crying, and calling out for someone to come and assist her in bringing back the escaping groom. Eventually, the groom stopped running and slumped down under a tree. It took Rosaria another twenty minutes to catch up with him.

"Come back," she called to him from where she was standing. "We shall be late for the wedding!"

But the groom did not seem to hear her. Rosaria decided to go and see what was wrong. And even when she stood in front of him, he seemed not to recognise her.

"What is the matter?" Rosaria asked in a concerned tone. "Every one must be waiting for you at church!"

Still he did not answer. In fact he was now heaving, and something seemed to be tugging at him, jerking him from one side to another.

Rosaria began screaming, hoping someone would hear her and come to her assistance. When it was apparent that no one was coming to rescue them, she began running back to the parish to go and inform Father Marcel. By the time she reached the church, every one was in a tantrum. They were looking for Rosaria to come and stand in her place so that she would escort the bride to church. They all believed the groom was already seated in church waiting for the bride. She broke the strange news to them and immediately a search team was dispatched to go and bring back the groom. He was still unable to talk but after some rest, he told them that he had no idea how he had gone up the hill. The wedding was conducted late in the evening.

After some days, the senior wife who had been chased away claimed responsibility of castingt the spell which had temporarily paralysed the groom on his wedding day.

***

The special bond which existed between Rosaria and Father Marcel grew by leaps and bounds. They were constantly in each other's company and whenever Father Marcel was too weak to get out of bed, Rosaria never left his bedside. Rosaria was a special child, Father Marcel always thought.

Her birth had been surrounded by mystery which up to now he had failed to resolve. It had been established that Marina had gotten pregnant while still at his orphanage, under his care, his and Sister Bernadette's. They had failed in their duty- no, he had failed to play his role of guardian and protector of the little, vulnerable and traumatised orphan he had brought back from Rwanda. He would never forgive himself or the villain who had caused Marina such suffering as if she had not already had her share of it.

One day, he had asked Sister Bernadette if she had any clue as to who Rosaria's father was, but she had answered in the negative, and so had Matayo when he had asked him. But Father Marcel had this creeping feeling that the two were trying to hide something from him.

Maybe it was high time he intensified his search to find Rosaria's father. Now that his illness was catching up with him, and Sister Bernadette's arthritis was becoming worse, who was going to take over Rosaria? Not her mother, not yet. Father Marcel did not want to push her into taking over her daughter if she was not yet ready to do it. What was important now was for Marina to forge a new life.

***

"Father, look," Rosaria said excitedly one day, pointing at Father Marcel's part of the forearm which was not covered by the heavy sweater he wore, "your skin is turning black! Just like ours. Isn't that wonderful!"

Father Marcel looked down at his arms. The skin around them was flaky and had began to peel off. There was also a visible brown tinge which Rosaria called 'black'.

"It is the sickness, Rosaria," he said quietly, "it does that to the skin."

"What's the name of the sickness, Father?" Rosaria asked rather seriously.

Father Marcel smiled at her, "It's too complicated for your little mind," he answered.

"No, tell me, maybe I would be able to help."

"It is called Chronic Pyelonephritis," he said, grimacing from the pangs of back pain which seemed to have intensified in the last one week. "This disease," he continued talking in the same quiet tone as if he was talking to himself, "gradually destroys the kidneys and very soon, I won't be able to walk."

There was a catch in his voice and Rosaria looked up at him, her little face creased with worry.

"Does that mean you are going to die?" she asked, tears forming in her eyes.

"Yes, Rosaria. We all have to die at one time if we want to see the kingdom of God."

"But I don't want you to die! Who will look after me?" She was now crying and Father Marcel took her in his arms and hugged her tightly.

"Don't worry, God will take care of you. And remember your parents love you very much; they will be able to take care of you," he said, trying to hold back his own tears without much success.

Chapter Two

When Marina eventually arrived at the orphanage, it was like a 'homecoming for her. She felt strangely at home. It was like coming back to familiar surroundings. The Orphanage had not changed much in the five years she had been away. The only unusual thing one noticed the moment one walked into the compound was the absence of Father Marcel's agile figure.

They sat for a long time without saying anything. They were seated in Father Marcel's bedroom and she was holding his frail hands in hers. His eyes were sunken and his skin flushed from the pain in his back.

It had taken Marina another year to go and visit her daughter as she had promised Mrs Magezi. Rosaria, she soon found out, was stunning at five. Her hair was curly and her skin was still as chocolate brown as the day she was born.

"How is Sister Bernadette?" Marina asked, turning her attention to Father Marcel.

"Holding her own. It is arthritis, you know. At times it gets bad and she has to stay in bed. But today...I don't know, I haven't seen her-maybe she is at the farm..." his voice trailed off and Marina could see that it was quite an effort for him to talk.

She glanced at Rosaria sitting on her lap and stroked her curly hair tenderly. She looked up at her too, and smiled.

"You love her very much, don't you?" Father Marcel asked softly, his voice barely audible.

"Yes," Marina answered quietly. "I have missed her, Father," she whispered, the tears coming to her eyes. It was difficult to imagine that Rosaria was the baby she had left behind five years ago.

"Father, has she come to take me away," Rosaria asked, turning to

Father Marcel.

He in turn looked at Marina, wanting her to answer the question herself.

"Yes," Marina answered. " But not today, sweetheart. I will come back again and take you with me."

"I want to go with you, now," Rosaria said. "Father Marcel said he is going to die; who will look after me?"

"He won't die. And I promise I will come back and take you," she said patiently, knowing it was a promise she had to keep.

"How are the other girls?" Marina asked, trying to change the subject

"They are fine. But most of those you were with are no longer here. Most of them got married, the others left on their own free will...maybe Stella Maris, she is here..."

"Stella Maris?" Marina asked excitedly. "But I thought she was in Hoima!"

"Well, yes, she was. Actually she was married to a catechist there, but she is here now. I'm sure she would like to see you too."

"Father, you mean Auntie Stella? I will go and call her," Rosaria said, jumping off her mother's lap.

Stella Maris came promptly. She gazed at her old friend and began giggling. Then in another minute, they were locked in a warm embrace.

"My God, Marina, when did you come?" she asked when she had managed to disentangle herself from Marina's tight grip.

"Just about an hour ago. And you, what are you doing here? I thought you were in Hoima!"

"I was. But...well...I'm here now."

"Well, you look...different. I mean, you look good." Marina added, noticing her friends discomfort.

"You too. You have gained a lot of weight! Are you married?"

"No." Marina answered with a laugh. "You?"

"No. I mean not any more." Both girls laughed.

"Let's go out for a walk," Marina said, noting that there was something she was not telling her. "I guess I should stretch my legs after the long journey, and well, look around my old home," she added.

Once outside, Marina asked her friend to tell her about her life after she had left her in Hoima about three years ago.

"There isn't much to tell, Marina," she answered in a sad tone. "After you left, I became very lonely. So when this man came along and suggested that we could get married, I accepted."

"So?" Marina prompted gently.

"He was a nice man, a catechist. But then I could not give him children," Stella Maris ended.

"So you left him? But if he was-"

"He chased me away," Stella Maris interrupted her before she could finish. Her voice was charged with emotion and Marina thought it better not to push her. She was getting depressed by the sad news at the orphanage. Every one seemed to be in pain, both physical and emotional.

"I wish I could also go away," Stella Maris surprised her by saying. "I don't want to live here again, everything has changed...all my friends are gone..."

"Don't worry," Marina tried to console her friend, "everything will be fine."

But she could see that Stella Maris would need more than just mere words to console her. She needed understanding, love, material support, to help her cope with the tragedy which had befallen her.

"Have you seen Matayo yet?" Stella Maris asked, changing the subject.

Marina turned away, feeling like her friend had hit her.

"No," she snapped back, "and I don't want to."

"I was only asking. He is so fond of Rosaria, you know, his wife too, and the kids. Actually she fits in there like she is one of them!"

Marina kept quiet. For a moment, she thought her friend was only trying to be insensitive, but then she realised that Stella Maris did not know the whole story. When they lived together in Hoima, she did not confided in her.

They were quiet for some time. Each engrossed in her own thoughts. Surprisingly, after many years of being apart, they could not find much to talk about.

"I think I'm tired," Marina announced, wanting to get away. "I will go in and rest, we shall talk more tomorrow."

Stella Maris did not stop her. She simply watched her as she walked towards Father Marcel's residence.

The following day, Marina did not see her friend. No one seemed to know where she was, but Marina guessed that she was only trying to avoid her.

Two days later, she left for the city promising to come back and take Rosaria. It was the only logical thing to do under the circumstances. With both Father Marcel and Sister Bernadette bed-ridden, who was going to look after her. She had not seen Matayo during her visit. She knew he had deliberately avoided her.

But if she had to take Rosaria, she also had to find a home to keep her. She could not add another burden onto the Magezis.

***

Back in the city, Marina could be seen in George's company frequently. Nonetheless, Mrs Magezi was surprised when she announced that she was getting married to George in a few months time.

"Honey, have you thought about this seriously? I mean you don't seem to be..."

"I'm doing the right thing, Aunt," Marina answered.

"Well, if it's what you want..."

When Mrs Magezi went to talk to her husband about her fears, she was surprised by his reaction.

"I thought you were the one encouraging her from the very beginning?" he said.

"I know, but come to think of it, I don't think George is the right man for her."

Mr Magezi smiled inwardly. His wife was behaving like a typical mother, afraid of losing her last born to a man. Aloud he said, "Why do you say that?"

"Well, I don't think he is. He is..."

"You see. You can't even think of a possible reason to disqualify the young man. Let him be," her husband said.

Chapter Three

Marina first noticed him one morning as they ate breakfast. She had seen him before in the company of her husband and their friends but like the others, Marina had no interest in him. But she knew that his name was Dee. They were all the same to her: self-centred, pompous men, who acted with a high-handedness which irritated her.

To keep peace in the house, she had to pretend that she enjoyed their company. Neither could she keep track of them. They were simply too many. They all claimed to be her husband's friends, and he pretended to like them all. Well, Marina knew better. For the last one year she had been married to George, she had come to learn that he loved no one except himself.

That morning, as they sat at the enormous dining table having breakfast, Marina noticed this youngish man. His head was buried in a newspaper and he continuously sipped at his coffee .

"Bring some food for Dee," her husband said, addressing Marina. She was about to get up when she caught Dee's eye. He shook his head slightly.

"Marina," her husband said again, raising his voice, "I said bring-"

"No, thank you, George," Dee interjected, "It's just coffee for me today. "

Marina was taken aback by the deep drawl of his voice. Somehow, it did not fit in with his age.

"Eat some food, man, it's good for your soul," George insisted. But Dee only smiled and shook his head.

The other men at the table continued talking, but Dee never said another word. He was deeply engrossed in the newspaper he was reading.

Marina was used to their obscene talk. Almost every day, they came to her house in the wee hours, dead drunk, expecting to eat the heavy breakfast which they knew she normally prepared for her husband. Most of them were unmarried and sometimes even spent the night at her house with their girlfriends, which was what they called the girls they picked up from the dancing places they went to. These girls never gave Marina a hand as she prepared breakfast because in most cases, they were in bed up to noon.

At first Marina had not paid much attention to what George's friends and their women were subjecting her to. She had two live-in maids who did most of the housework. But later, when her husband insisted that he wanted her to cook all his meals and chased away the maids, she began to feel the stress.

She had complained to her husband, who had only laughed in her face and said that an African woman was supposed to cater not only for her husband's needs but for those of his whole clan as well, and in this case, his friends.

The complaint later ended in a fight and Marina ran away and went back to the Magezis. After a few days, George came to apologise and Mrs Magezi encouraged and persuaded Marina to go back with her husband who promised to bring back the maids and control his friends' visits.

But the same pattern began all over again barely a month after the fight and he chased away the maids on some flimsy excuse. Marina was now ashamed of going back to Mrs Magezi and complaining about the same thing.

I will find a way of handling it, she told herself. In the meantime, she did what she could to manage as one person and kept a deaf ear whenever her husband complained that his meals were late or the house was not clean. Marina often wondered what these men did exactly, and who they were. They never seemed to have offices or jobs, but she knew that they discussed their 'business' in either Goerge's office or at their home, in the privacy of her husband's study.

At times, she would catch some of their conversation which always centred on car deals and money transactions. All she knew was that they had been George's buddies for a long time and he always talked of how deep their friendship run and how sincere and committed they all were to it, ready to stick out their necks for each other.

Marina sat listening to their talk now. They talked about the university girls who had 'detoothed' them the previous night by drinking their booze and later disappearing into thin air.

"Take this girl for example," one of them called Mufalume began, "I went through the right channels to get her, and..."

"What do you mean by the right channels?" another one called Boss asked.

"Well, I paid these boys who are always hanging out in the guild canteen and who know which girls are ready to go for a quickie for a few shillings. The girl came to me quite willingly and first we went to Grand Imperial Hotel for dinner, then ended up at *Ange Noir* and danced till 2 p.m. I thought that was enough, and I demanded for *ebyaffe*

"She assured me that her roommate was not round so we could use her room in Mary Stuart Hall. Well, after I had spent a fortune at Imperial, I decided that sleeping in a free room and using free water and electricity wouldn't be bad at all. Anyhow, we reached Mary Stuart and she opened the car door. 'I will make the bed warm as you lock up the car,' she said sweetly."

"Don't tell me that you stupidly believed her?" Boss interrupted him.

"How was I to know that she was pulling my leg?" Mufalume said defensively.

"She must have seen how daft you were," Boss continued mercilessly, "otherwise -"

"Don't you sit there calling me daft!" Mufalume burst out.

"Quit your nonsense, you two," George came in authoritatively. "Who among you has never been 'detoothed' by these smart girls of Makerere?"

"Let the one who has never sinned throw the first stone," another of their friends said. They all laughed and resumed their breakfast.

"George," Mufalume now asked, changing the topic, "why do you think Charlie named his discotheque *Ange Noir*, what does it mean ?"

George shrugged indifferently but did not answer.

"Boss, do you know why," Mufalume asked, now turning to him.

"No," Boss answered.

"Black angel," Marina blurted out before she could stop herself.

Her husband turned and stared at her. "How could you know that ?" he asked coldly.

"Is that right?" Mufalume said turning to Marina with admiration in his eyes.

"Of course not," her husband continued coldly. "She wouldn't know it. Besides, she has never been there."

Marina would never forgive herself for shooting off her mouth like that. She knew that her husband never wanted her to make any form of comment whenever his friends were around. She would never have given a damn what they thought of her, but suddenly, she was embarrassed for

138

being reprimanded in front of Dee. Somehow, she wanted him to respect her.

She now turned and looked at him. He had put down the newspaper and was staring at her with a mixture of awe and confusion in his eyes. Her husband stood up angrily and left the table. Moments later, the other four men joined him outside.

Marina began to clear the table. She was boiling with anger, both at herself and at her husband for having humiliated her. She always tried to keep clear of her husband's anger, especially when she knew that he was mad at her because of what had transpired between them the previous night. He had come back drunk and demanded sex from her. As usual, she was not receptive enough. Sometimes he never came back at all, and Marina knew that on such nights he slept with other women. She did not feel anything, except maybe relief that at least he would not bother her for at least two days.

"Where did you learn French from ?"

The heavy drawl made Marina jump; she had not even realised that Dee was still sitting at the table.

"I just know a little," she answered evasively.

He nodded his head, but there was no telling whether he was satisfied with the answer or not. She reached for his cup but he put a restraining hand on it. There was still some coffee in it.

"It must have gone cold. I will get you some hot coffee if you like ," Marina said.

Dee shook his head. He drained the cold coffee in one gulp and handed the cup to Marina. "Thanks, ma'am," he said quietly. Again Marina was struck by that heavy drawl. He did not leave the table immediately but continued reading his newspaper.

She finished clearing the table and took the dishes to the kitchen. There was a small partitioning window between the kitchen and the dining room and Marina peeped at Dee through it.

He was smoking a cigarette and his eyes seemed to be intently fixed on an imaginary object, his head inclined to one angle as if he was in deep thought. He had brown eyes and his head was completely shaven leaving the scalp shining. He had an extended forehead which made him look as if he had gone bald prematurely.

After a while, he stood up and joined the others outside.

Marina was intrigued by him. Who was he and what was his real name?

Chapter Four

Dee continued coming to their house, mainly for breakfast, and every time Marina saw him, she found herself lost in his mystery. He never said much. Even when his friends talked about their favourite topics of women and said funny things, he only smiled and continued reading his newspaper.

Somehow he did not fit in with her husband's other friends. He looked quite intelligent and was much younger than the rest. He also dressed modestly, always in simple pinstriped short-sleeved shirts and black or navy blue trousers, unlike the other men who were always over-dressed in bright, shouting colours, or white trousers, gold chains and gold-rimmed spectacles. Marina found their smartness irritating.

The only topic which seemed to stimulate Dee was when the men discussed the Rwanda genocide. Only then would his face show some interest and he would argue long and vehemently until the other men gave up.

"They are all bloody killers, the whole bunch of them. Whether they are Tutsi or Hutu, they are all bloodthirsty," Marina recalled one of those heated arguments she had witnessed as she sat watching television.

"Let them kill and finish each other off," another one chipped in. "The only thing I don't understand is why Uganda is trying to meddle in their affairs which don't concern us!"

"What do you mean that Uganda should not interfere?" Dee interjected. "You want us to just watch as those murderers kill the innocent Tutsi?" His voice was rising in anger. "Just like the international community which is totally indifferent to these killings taking place on the surface of this earth, as if the people being killed are mere rats? And

140

look at France, offering assistance to the murderers!"

"But what about the UN? Honestly, I thought they should interfere," another man joined in.

"You think it's not aware of the amount of violence taking place?" Dee asked in annoyance. "But what are they doing to stop it? Instead, it has reduced its size of peacekeeping troops in Rwanda, claiming that it is too expensive to maintain! Personally, I feel there is no love lost; let them take away their good-for-nothing troops. After all, they even abandon the very people they came to save and instead rescue the foreigners!"

There was silence for a moment. Dee looked like he was ready to hit someone.

"Dee," George now asked placatingly, "who do you think assassinated the President?"

"Carlos," Dee answered quietly.

"Carlos?" the men asked, surprised.

"Who is he?" George asked again.

Dee laughed thinly before replying. "It's a pity you don't read papers. You mean you don't know Carlos, Carlos the Jackal?"

George looked blankly at Dee and the latter laughed loudly. "Anyhow, Carlos was acting on orders," Dee continued.

"Whose orders?" George asked

"Of the members of CDR."

"But that was the party the President had just formed!"

"Yes, the members were angered by the conciliatory reforms that were being granted to the Tutsi refugees as a result of the Arusha Accord."

Heavy silence fell on the men again as they digested the information Dee had just given them.

"These Tutsi, can't they run and hide, for God's sake? How can they stay there waiting for death to come to them?" one man commented.

"There is nowhere for them to hide," Dee answered quietly, a faraway look in his eyes. "Their enemies hunt for them everywhere. They even cut down the trees and burn the bushes where they suspect the Tutsi could be hiding. They also burn down the houses. Others who decide to take sanctuary in the temples of God are given away by the very custodians of faith and hope: the priests and nuns. They alert the Hutu, and they come and mow down the Inyenzi with machetes and clubs, and God knows what else. The bellies of pregnant women are slit open and their husbands are made to eat the foetuses before they are bayoneted themselves. They say they don't want to make the same mistake their predecessors made in 1959 when they let the children go free. The same children have now re-organised themselves and they have gone back to fight the government.

"They force the Tutsi to kill their own kin, so that they can also have blood on their hands. And," Dee continued, his voice taking on a dull monotone, " the men pay the murderers money so that they can kill their loved ones, wives and kids, decently. If you don't pay, your wife is slain right in front of you in the most ghastly manner. The murderers pierce her with a sharp object through the vagina until she dies. But if you pay well, she is only gang-raped first, then shot once through the head."

Dee had stopped talking, but no one seemed to have noticed. Marina was crying quietly, remembering too vividly what Dee had just described. In a rare display of tenderness, George stood up and went to her. He placed a comforting hand on her shoulders and slowly led her to their bedroom. Dee, too, stood up and went to stand by the window. After some time, he left with the other men.

***

The following day, Marina was having a shower when she heard a car stop in the driveway. She glanced through the window and saw her husband's red Ferrari. She quickly dried herself and stepped out of the bathtub. She knew her husband must have forgotten something because it was hardly twenty minutes since he had left. She also knew that he had left in a sour mood after their quarrel that morning. The next thing she knew he would be barking at her to hurry and find whatever he had forgotten.

She wrapped a towel around her herself and went downstairs.

At first she did not see him. When she did, she felt hot embarrassment wash over her and she wished she was more decently clothed. Dee just stood there, a lazy smile on his face, his big brown eyes dancing with laughter.

"Where is George ?" Marina asked, trying to cover her embarrassment .

"In his office," Dee answered in his quiet drawl.

"But I thought it was him, I mean the car," Marina continued in a panicky voice.

George never allowed anyone to drive that car. He was obsessed with the fact that, apart from the rich Indian tycoon who owned a string of hotels in the city, no one else owned a Ferrari in Uganda. And so he wanted people to see him and only him driving the car and know that he was the second richest man in Uganda, after the Indian.

"Well, I guess I will go back upstairs," Marina said, feeling awkward at having to stand there half-naked talking to Dee.

Dee shrugged and made no effort to move; it seemed he was enjoying her embarrassment. The sad face from last night was gone and his eyes had a light in them. He thrust his hands in his pockets and came out with a cigarette and lighter. He lit the cigarette and took one long puff. He watched Marina through a haze of smoke, his eyes slightly closed.

"Ah...did you want anything ?" Marina asked him, feeling furious.

"Yes, ma'am," he answered coolly. "I forgot my newspaper on your dining table."

"Then you can get it," Marina said , her voice rising. she angry note in it could not be missed.

Dee stared at her quietly. He threw the butt of the cigarette on the floor and ground it with the heel of his shoe. Then he strode past her and went to the dining room, picked up the newspaper and came to stand in front of her.

He took one step toward her and brought his face level to hers. She could smell his male odour mixed with tobacco: it smelt delightfully sweet.

She felt a shiver run through her and a warmth settle in her loins. She was tinglingly aware of his presence. She felt Dee's hands on her bare shoulders, yet she did not push them away. She felt exhilaration flowing through her whole body. Her eyes began to mist over and her legs weakened.

Dee gently pushed the towel from her and it fell down with a soft thud. He drew her naked body close to his chest and held her there. Then without warning, his mouth closed over hers, parting her lips with his tongue. Marina opened her lips wider, responding to Dee's kiss uncontrollably. He deepened the kiss, sucking out the air from her lungs, his tongue teasing , making tiny circles in her mouth. Marina could not control herself anymore. She cried out in a small protesting voice.

He released her slowly and reluctantly but his eyes never left hers. He bent down and picked up the towel, then clumsily tried to wrap it around her waist.

Marina opened her mouth to speak, but he placed his index finger on her lips, silencing her. He walked to the door, stopped and looked back at her, then he was gone.

Marina just stood there, unable to move. She heard the car start up, then reverse noisily and drive away.

He is gone, Marina thought in bewilderment. He was actually here, in this room, and he kissed me, but now he is gone! She tried to convince herself that this was a dream, and that she was just imagining or making up things.

Dee! Oh my God, Dee! What had he done, or rather, what had she let him do to her. She closed her eyes and felt his hands on her body and the sensation she had felt and she smelled a whiff of his perfume which was still lingering in the sitting room.

Jesus,what is happening to me, she thought frightened. She seemed to realise that she was still standing there, naked. She gathered all her strength and walked back upstairs. She slumped on the bed and lay there, drained of all energy.

What had happened to her this afternoon? She had never felt like that before. Dee. Who was he? Who was this man who could make her feel like this.

She did not realise that she was crying. The tears just rolled down her cheeks, uncontrolled. She must have drifted off to sleep because she woke with a start and found the whole bedroom covered in darkness. She glanced at the clock beside the bed; it was seven o'clock.

I must not stay here, I must go to the kitchen and prepare dinner, she told herself many times, trying to find the justification to leave the bed.

***

The following day, Dee did not come for breakfast, nor did he come the next day. Marina could not explain how she felt. Relieved on one hand and disappointed on the other. That dull aching was still there. She missed him. Dee had kissed her. What did that mean? That he loved her, wanted her? What about her own reactions to the kiss, to Dee's advances? How could she explain that? I am a married woman, married to George, the man I don't love and will never love, she kept on reminding herself.

And who is Dee? Another philanderer like her husband and all his friends? He was not a particularly handsome man, but he was attractive. And maybe a bit unique, even weird. If he was not reading a newspaper, he would be staring at something, intently, as if he wanted to memorise the smallest details about it and later convey his findings to someone else, or report to someone else.

Report! The word seemed to trigger something in Marina's mind. Reporter, could it be that Dee was a reporter? A newsman? Was that why he seemed to be listening and observing all the time? What the blue blazes was a pressman doing in her husband's company? Maybe she was wrong, maybe Dee was a car dealer, just like all her husband's friends.

She tried hard to get him out of her system, but she could not. Wherever she turned, she saw his brown smiling big eyes staring at her, mocking her, challenging her, trying to force the truth out of her that she was actually missing him. She threw all her energy into housework and made sure that all her daytime hours were fully occupied, leaving her no time to day-dream. She once caught her husband staring at her strangely.

"What's got into you these days?" he asked her.

"What do you mean?" she asked, feigning ignorance.

"You are just...just ...I don't know how to put it."

Marina ignored him and did not reply. Her husband rarely talked to her, or rather they could never sustain a meaningful conversation without it degenerating into an ugly argument. Marina tried to remember when they had last talked as husband and wife. Was it after that first night following their wedding?

Their wedding! Marina always thought about it with loathing. She had sat through it stoically, neither happy nor sad, listening to the droning voice of the priest. Later, she had said her vows in a quiet tone and the priest had to constantly ask her to raise her voice. Neither Father Marcel nor Sister Bernadette could come for the wedding. The only people at her side were Mr and Mrs Magezi.

Her husband had been understanding , or so she had thought. He did not invite his own parents because he did not want Marina to feel bereft. The reception party had also been a small affair, conducted at their house and attended only by close friends. Then they had flown to Nairobi for their honeymoon. That night, she could not bring herself to respond to her husband's sexual advances. He had been highly aroused and he was very impatient with her.

"What is it?" he had asked, barely able to conceal his irritation.

"Nothing," Marina had answered quickly. Then he had tried again, this time forcibly entering her. She had squirmed and tried to push him away but he was too aroused to stop and just continued pounding her.

The next morning, she had avoided looking at him, and that night, and all the other nights which followed, it had been the same story. Him wanting her to be all ready and accommodative, and she all tensed up and dry.

Their sex life was an instant disaster. She could never have sex with him. Every time he was on top of her, the pictures of Matayo, and the colonel who had raped her mother would flash through her mind.

"If you were a virgin, I would understand," her husband had burst out one night. "But you have ever eaten goods with some other man and here you are trying to act like an angel."

When all that failed, he went to Mrs Magezi to tell them how their 'daughter' was behaving. Mrs Magezi called Marina to talk to her.

"Marina, you must understand your responsibilities as a married woman," she said to her.

"He hurts me, he is big!" Marina had answered defensively.

"Is that so?" Mrs Magezi asked in an alarmed voice. "You mean he is... He is...I mean too big?"

"I think so," Marina answered in embarrassment. She hated to lie to Mrs Magezi, or even to talk to her about this kind of thing. Yet she knew that George hurt her deliberately.

She had one day landed on a picture of a young beautiful girl in George's personal drawer.

"Who is this?" she had asked before she could stop herself and was surprised when George answered her question.

"Her name was Lisa."

"Was?" Marina asked sharply.

"Yes, she was once my girlfriend but she is deceased now." George gave the information without any feeling and Marina was forced to glance at him to see if he was serious. His face was like stone.

Marina looked closely at the picture of the dead girl: her eyes were incredibly brown; they reminded her of another person with similar eyes and she almost said so, but quickly caught herself.

"What did she die of?" she asked instead.

"Car accident," George replied quietly, his tone still devoid of any feelings. "She did bad things to me, Marina," he said as a way of explanation. "At first, I wanted to punish every woman I met for her sins, I wanted them to pay on her behalf but..."he shrugged and did not continue.

But Marina knew that she was the one paying for Lisa's sins because whenever he had sex with her, he seemed as if he was punishing her, wanting to hurt her. She wondered what Lisa had done to him.

Another time she had seen another picture of another woman. This time, she had not bothered to ask him. There was an inscription at the back of the picture which read: *"My darling, I want to be your prostitute when we are in bed, your chef when I'm in the kitchen, and your queen when we go out."*

Marina did not know whether to laugh or cry. Is this what George wanted his women to be?

He always made sure that she dressed smartly, going to great lengths to buy her all the latest designs. It was like competition between her and the wives of his other friends, to see who dressed more expensively. But Marina did not need the clothes, after all there were very few outings for her.

"Marina," Mrs Magezi now asked, bringing her back to the present, "tell me, if you had no feelings for him, then why did you marry him?"

"I...lov..." she was about to say that she loved her husband but caught herself in time. It wasn't fair to tell her aunt another lie. She was only trying to help her.

Why had she actually married George? She thought to herself before replying. To be able to give Rosaria a father, a home, security for food and a decent education. Or was she trying to run away from...who? Herself. Was she trying to find love.

"I don't know," she answered truthfully. "At first, well, I thought that he was a...good...man...I mean, about sex. He never used to demand for it like he does now."

"It is because you are his wife now, Marina," Mrs Magezi said gently. "You have to have sex with him!"

Marina nodded.

"Do you understand?"

"I will try," Marina promised.

But she knew her husband was taking on lover after lover. He now accused her of being barren or taking some form of contraceptive. Their fights were becoming more frequent. She had decided not to bring Rosaria into such a home. She was still better off where she was.

But now she had learnt not to fight him; that way, it was less painful. Dee had awakened the feelings Marina had not imagined existed in her. He had made her feel like a woman, a woman like all the others who could respond to a man's sexual arousal.

Chapter Five

Marina looked through the window at the grey sky and the wet ground, but she was not deterred by it: she was determined to go out. The melancholy foggy April Sunday had started with a promise of rain. The sky had finally released its waters in a violent downpour. The house felt like a cage, and she, like a caged animal. She knew she had to go out.

She was about to open the front door when the phone rang. She cursed silently, knowing it must be her husband. On such occasions, he was always armed with all sorts of excuses to explain why he had not returned the previous night. She could not understand why he bothered to explain anymore, they both knew where he slept when he did not return. She hoped he was not going to tell her to make his breakfast.

"Yes," she said impatiently into the phone.

"Good morning, ma'am," the heavy, lazy drawl at the other end of the line caught her off guard and she held her breath before answering.

"Hello?" Dee was talking again. "Are you there?"

"Yes, yes, how are you doing, Dee?" she asked hoping he would not detect the breathlessness in her voice.

"I'm doing pretty fine, ma'am, and how about you?"

He sounded like he was in a jolly mood, Marina noted before answering. "I'm fine. Would you like to talk to George? I'm sorry he is not in," she added quickly.

"I know," he said quietly. "It's not George I want to talk to, it's you."

"Ah, well, I'm afraid I'm going out now, maybe..."

"Perfect," Dee interrupted her. "Then we can meet at Sabrina Club on Bombo Road. You know where it is, don't you?"

"No," Marina said almost shouting," I can't meet you there."

"Why not?" Dee asked matter-of-factly.

"Well...well, because, I just can't; you must understand."

"No I don't, you tell me," Dee shot back.

"Well..., I just can't ," Marina said, a note of annoyance creeping into her voice. "What do you want to talk to me about, anyway? If you have anything to say, you know where I live." With that, she slammed down the receiver. She was breathing heavily and had to lean on the wall for support. She was angry at the way Dee was trying to assert himself. Just because I let him kiss me does not give him a license to call me any time he wants and expect me to jump, she thought angrily. She opened the door and let herself out.

The heavy downpour had subsided to a light drizzle and one could afford to walk in it without getting drenched. She reached the taxi stage but there was no taxi in sight. It was not surprising being a Sunday, and a rainy one at that, she thought. She sat on a bench and prepared to wait. The cold wind was blowing at her from all sides and her legs were freezing. She did not even know where she was heading to, so long as it was out of her home.

After fifteen minutes, she decided that she was not going to wait anymore. She was about to cross the road when she saw a vehicle stop next to her.

"Get in, ma'am," Dee said, putting out his head.

Marina stared at him startled. The driver behind Dee's car was hooting and shouting obscenities at them.

"Get in," Dee said more urgently.

Marina hesitated. How had Dee found out that she would be here?

The driver behind them had got out of his car and from the look on his face, he seemed ready to engage them in a fist-fight.

"Please get in," Dee said, opening the car door more widely. Marina jumped in and he sped off in the direction of the city. He drove for some time in silence. The air from the cold wind outside blew in her face and she shivered involuntarily. Dee glanced at her and said, "Are you feeling cold?"

"No," Marina snapped, "I feel like someone has been stalking me."

Dee smiled but he did not say anything. Nonetheless, he pressed a button on his side of the window and the window on Marina's side went up.

"How did you know I would be there?" she asked him.

"Simple," Dee answered easily. "I know you don't drive, so when you said you were going out, I suspected you had to go and catch a taxi."

She was silent for a moment. His reasoning seemed quite logical but still she was not sure. In any case, he had saved her from walking back home in the cold.

"Where are we going?" she asked after sometime.

"Home, " he answered automatically. "I'm taking you home, ma'am. Isn't that where you were going ?"

"But you are headed..." Marina began to say.

"I know, I just want to pick something I forgot at home, then I will deliver you safe and sound at your house. Don't you trust me?" he added smiling at her. She did not respond and only stared out of the window.

"I won't be long ," he said when he finally got to his house. He jumped out and entered one of the semi-detached houses. Marina looked closely at the house; the other side seemed to be unoccupied. The verandah of the house which Dee had entered was littered with dry leaves and pieces of paper. The grass in the compound was overgrown and it was impossible to imagine that the house was inhabited.

Curiosity got the better of her and she got out of the car. She hoped to catch the inside of the house before Dee returned. Maybe I will learn something about this strange man, she thought as she neared the window. As she reached the front door, it opened and Dee stood there.

"Oh, do you want to come in?" he asked, surprise showing on his face.

"Ah, not really, I just wanted to...to...stretch my legs," Marina ended vaguely, feeling like a small child who has been caught committing some crime.

"It's okay if you want to come in," Dee said lightly, moving out of the doorway. "Come in," he pressed her when she stood there hesitating.

He opened the door wider and led her inside. The sitting room, if it could be called that, was tiny and devoid of any furniture. Marina looked around vaguely, not knowing what to say. Dee was watching her quietly, saying nothing. Then her eyes fell on a big potted plant at the far corner. She walked up to it and gently stroked its leaves.

"My friend gave it to me," Dee answered Marina's unasked question. "It's called a money plant," he went on to explain. "When you are broke, it withers, and when you are loaded, it thrives." He laughed and Marina laughed with him, breaking the tension which had been hanging between them.

"Here, let me show you the rest of the house," he said, leading her to the kitchen.

"Why don't you buy some chairs?" Marina asked, as they stood in the doorway of the kitchen.

"What for?" Dee answered shrugging. "I'm never here and I hardly receive any visitors."

The kitchen, Marina noted, was simple but tidy, with a few items of cutlery and a hot plate standing near the wall. They moved on and passed through the corridor. On the left side was a tiny bedroom with a single bed in it without a mattress, and opposite was the bathroom, but it was partly closed and Marina did not open the door. Then right ahead was the bigger bedroom.

"This is my simple abode," he said, smiling as he reached for the door. Marina glanced inside; there was a world of difference here.

The bed was huge and it was covered with a beautiful bedspread which was done in soft design. The floor was covered with a thick rug and beside the legs of the bed, were two loudspeakers. There was a framed photograph on the small table beside the bed. Marina picked it up and examined it closely.

" Is this you ?" she asked him.

" No, that is my brother," Dee answered.

"He looks very much like you. Is he older than you?"

"Yes," Dee answered. But he did not offer anymore information.

Marina stood there awkwardly, not knowing what to do next.

As she was about to move from the bedroom, she felt rather than saw Dee walk behind her and wrap his arms around her body. He turned her slowly and she stood facing him, then he pulled her closer and his lips found hers.

All this while, Marina did not try to stop him and she briefly wondered why. Dee's mouth was searching hers, trying to force it open with his tongue. But this time, the kiss was not as gentle as the first time he had kissed her; this time, he was demanding, more passionate. Without any warning, Dee lifted her off the floor and placed her on the bed. Only then did Marina try to resist.

"Shhhhh ," Dee hushed her, placing his forefinger on her lips. He began to undress her, slowly but urgently, removing one garment at a time. When he reached her underwear, Marina put up a feeble protest but Dee could not be stopped now. He was moving faster, his hands like those of an experienced hunter skinning an animal.

Soon she was lying on the bed completely naked. He gazed at her, mesmerised. "Jesus, you are a beautiful girl ," he said breathlessly.

His strong hands began stroking her naked body, exploring each curve as if he wanted to commit it to memory. Her nipples began to harden. Dee noticed them and slowly bent down and took one hardened nipple in his mouth, then the other. Marina tried to push him away, afraid that she would not be able to take in all the pleasure she was experiencing. Dee lifted his head and the expression on his face seemed to say, 'Don't even try.' She lay back and closed her eyes.

A throbbing sensation was beginning to grow inside her and an animal-like sound escaped her. Dee released her breasts and began planting short, quick kisses on her forehead, chest, then stomach, going down, down, until his tongue found a mound of damp warmth which was her womanhood, and then he began teasing, exploring.

Marina was aroused to the highest heights. She arched herself towards the arousing tongue, urging Dee to move even faster. Dee suddenly stopped and withdrew his tongue. Marina let out a small protesting sound. Dee looked at her, and his face feigning surprise asked archly. "What is it, ma'am?"

In answer Marina reached out with her hands and felt the pressure of his aroused manhood and guided it inside her. Dee seemed to have been waiting for exactly that. He made a swift movement and he was suddenly lying on top of her. With the force of his body, he drove himself inside her. He plunged deeper inside her and began moving faster, establishing a rhythm which Marina found herself joining in.

At one point, Marina felt on the verge of explosion and Dee must have sensed it too, because just then, he withdrew abruptly.

"No...oooo ," Marina screeched. Dee pulled himself on his elbows and glanced at her before laughter broke out at the corners of his mouth. He was teasing of course, wanting to know if she wanted more. Marina pulled him back and once again guided his manhood inside her. This time, Dee clutched her bare buttocks and began riding her, in and out, side ways, forth and backwards. Marina wrapped her legs around his heaving torso, imprisoning him there, not wanting him to move away this time.

Dee intensified the motion and with each movement, he drove deeper inside her. She felt the tremors begin to grow inside her; Dee felt them too and he held her more tightly. Then with one more thrust, they both exploded into a thousand shudders, heaving and lurching their bodies from side to side. Dee continued holding her until the tremors inside her body, and the low moaning sounds emanating from her subsided.

At first, she thought she was having a dream. Then she felt the damp, but warm sticky liquid trickling between her thighs and gingerly felt for its source; it was still hard. Only then did she believe what had happened to her.

Dee released her and pulled himself up, then went to the bathroom.

"Don't leave me," Marina whimpered after him. He came back wiping his face with a towel and sat on the bed. He pulled her over and made her sit on his lap as one would a baby. He lowered her body gently across his lap and slowly kissed her full on the mouth. Marina snuggled close to his warm body and relaxed her muscles. She closed her eyes and soon she was fast asleep.

Dee gently put her back in bed and got in beside her. He lit a cigarette and through a haze of smoke, stared at her serene sleeping face.

He felt an overwhelming urge to protect her.

Chapter Six

George had not returned when Marina got back to the house that evening and she thanked God for it. She just wished to be alone to try to reflect on her feelings and actions of that morning. She went straight to bed, not bothering to think what her husband would eat for dinner if he came back at all that night.

"You cannot go back to him," she remembered Dee telling her when she was leaving. "We cannot pretend that today never happened. It was too good to let it pass as a one-night stand."

Marina knew it was useless even thinking about it. Her decision was already made for her; she was married to George and that was that. But as days turned into weeks, Marina could not understand what was happening to her. What had happened between her and Dee was something she failed to comprehend. She felt light-headed, and drunk with love, or was it desire? She was constantly smiling and occasionally found herself laughing over nothing.

She knew she had to put a stop to it , but she had neither the energy nor the will to do so. She wished she could surrender her whole life to Dee and let him take control, and take her under his protective wing so that she need not have a care in the world. She also wanted them to have a repeat of what had taken place on that delightful morning.

As days went by, they continued making love at least three times a week. Their lovemaking was not as wild as the first time but it was always terrific and Marina never wanted it to end.

She always worried about the way Dee seemed to be careless about the whole affair and brushed off her insistence to take precautions as unnecessary. He never seemed to care whether her husband found out about them or not. Marina attributed this to Dee's careless nature because he never took anything seriously.

He continued coming to their house for breakfast and Marina found herself noticing small, silly, unimportant things about him. For example, she noticed that his nails were long and thin and that he constantly chewed on them. The palms of his hands were as black as soot, probably because he was a chain smoker. He was also left-handed. Whenever he was in deep thought, he tilted his head to one side, opened his mouth slightly, and closed his eyes. Dee also wore his trousers slightly above the waistline, which gave him a boyish look.

"What is going to happen to us?" Marina had asked him one day after they had made love.

"What do you want to happen ?" he had asked lazily, stretching his long legs in front of him.

"I don't know," Marina had answered truthfully.

"Well, I know. You only have to pack your bags and leave him. Come and live with me."

"But I couldn't do that!" Marina said astonished.

"Why not ?"

"Well, what would people say?"

"Damn the people!" he said harshly. "What have the people got to do with this? Look Marina," he said more quietly, "we love each other and there is nothing stopping us from living together. We could go away from here if you want."

"Dee, I can't just go off with you like that. I mean, I don't even know anything about you. Besides, you seem to forget that I'm a married woman!"

"Married indeed!" he snorted. "Look, Marina, you cannot fool me because I know what kind of man your husband is and what your so-called marriage is like. So let's get serious about this, I want you and I'm going to have you. Period."

Marina had not expected this turn of events. Somehow, she had always known that Dee could be aggressive and demanding if he wanted, but she had never expected him to be this blunt. Maybe it was time she got more serious about the whole affair, as Dee had suggested, and called it off.

"I have to go," she said abruptly, not wanting a confrontation with him now. "We shall talk about this tomorrow." She stood up to indicate that she was serious about what she was saying. Dee did not say anything but watched her as she walked away.

***

When Marina got back home that evening, she found George seated in the sofa, reading a newspaper. George never read newspapers and she knew he was merely pretending. He peeped at her over the newspaper, but said nothing. Marina was not in the mood to play 'good wife'. She removed her shoes and slumped in the chair opposite him stifling a yawn.

"Where the hell have you been ?" he asked her, and his tone was laced with anger.

She was caught off guard she almost replied 'With Dee' "I...I...was with..." her mind blacked out; she could not think of anything to say. If only she had anticipated finding her husband home, she would have been prepared with an array of lies to tell him. He was staring at her with a murderous look, his face twisted in anger, like a puff-adder about to strike.

"Don't play with fire," he warned dangerously, "because you know what will happen. It will burn you!" There was an edge in his voice which Marina had never heard before.

"I was with Aunt," Marina said. It was the first thing which came to her mind. The look in her husband's eyes had somehow ruffled her.

"Liar," he spat out, and Marina jumped. "You didn't have to think over that before you replied. Suppose I rang them now to find out? Then we would see about that little alibi of yours," he said, his eyes dancing dangerously with fury.

"Go ahead ," Marina answered with more confidence than she felt. She had recovered from the initial shock. Besides, she was tired of being kept on a short leash as if she was some kind of criminal. The man never allowed her to go anywhere!

"Well, well, it seems my dear angelic wife has finally got herself a lover to warm her bed in my absence! How interesting!" he said scornfully.

He stood up slowly and came to stand in front of her. He looked down at her with a sinister look and said with derision, "Who is he?"

Marina stared back at him blankly.

"Who is this little boyfriend of yours?" he was now screaming at her.

Does he really think that I'm going to admit something as horrendous as infidelity? Marina almost answered back but inwardly, she was shaken. Suppose...?

"I'm going to find out about him, then we shall see who the fool is," he said as he moved to the door.

"George," she called after him.

He looked back and waited. But Marina could not think of anything to say. He opened the door and let himself out.

Marina could not think of what to do immediately. She looked around the sitting room helplessly. Her eyes landed on the telephone and an idea came to her mind. I must warn Dee, she thought urgently. Her hands shook as she dialled Dee's number, praying that he would be at home. The phone rang six times before he picked it up and by that time Marina was a nervous wreck.

"Dee, he knows, he is coming for you," she said breathlessly into the phone. She was also crying.

"Hey, hey, calm down, sweetheart. Now honestly why are you cry-ing? Has somebody pinched your behind?" Dee replied indolently.

Marina smiled through her tears. "Dee, there is no time, can't you understand? That man is dangerous."

"Now, Marina, who is not a man?" Dee said in a wounded tone.

"Okay, I'm sorry, but Dee, you just don't know what he can do to you, he is very upset," Marina begged him.

"I'm quaking in my pants," Dee answered in a cool tone.

Marina almost slammed down the telephone. Sometimes Dee could be so infuriating. She did not need his machismo now, she needed him alive.

"Okay," he said more ardently now. "Stop panicking and listen to me very carefully."

Marina blew her nose loudly.

"Are you listening?" Dee asked impatiently.

"Yes," Marina answered, "I thought you'd never get serious."

"Well, I'm serious now. I want you to pack a small bag and leave that place. Go straight to Speke Hotel and use my name. Just say...you know where the hotel is, don't you?" Dee asked

"Of course I do," Marina answered irritably.

"Very well, just say that you are waiting for me and they will book you in a room. Then wait for me. Is that clear?"

"Yes" Marina answered uncertainly. She was dammed if she was going to follow his instructions.

"And Marina," Dee was talking to her again, "don't forget to bring your passport."

"My passport?" Marina asked incredulously.

"You heard me," Dee said before he hung up the phone.

Marina was momentarily dazed. She stood without moving for sometime. "I cannot do this," she said aloud, as if trying to convince herself. "But suppose..." The murderous look in George's eyes before he had left the house flashed in her mind and it seemed to spur her to action.

She rushed to their bedroom and pulled a suitcase from the top of the closet. She flung open the closet and stared at the many clothes filling it.

"Oh my God!" she moaned softly. What was she going to take and what could she leave? Well, she had to make a decision quite fast. She began throwing things indiscriminately into the suitcase and when it was full, she closed it. Then she pulled out the small drawer on the dressing table where she normally kept some money and her passport. She was ready to go.

***

He pressed hard on the accelerator and the powerful Ferrari surged forward, obeying its master's mood. He drove straight to the Magezis house.

At this time of the night, he hoped he would not interrupt their dinner.

Mrs Magezi opened the door for him. She took one look at him and guessed instantly that there was something terribly wrong.

"Is everything all right ?" she asked, alarmed.

George did not answer, he moved past her into the sitting room and slumped into a chair. Mrs Magezi followed him inside, now more alarmed than before.

"Have you seen Marina today?" George asked.

"No, is she...is she in trouble?" Mrs Magezi asked.

"Yes."

"Wha...t what has happened?" Mrs Magezi was already shaking in fear.

But George was not to be rushed. He looked at her calmly and said instead, "Look, Aunt, I'm not a fool, nor am I an infant. I know my wife is cheating on me."

Mrs Magezi stared at him in consternation. "Are you sure?"

"Positive, and I want to tell you that I'm not going to stand that kind of nonsense. In fact I want her to leave my house immediately."

"Look, George, I don't want you to rush into making any decisions you will later regret. I believe this is something we can all talk over,"

158

Mrs Magezi told him. She had now overcome the initial shock, and to her, this did not seem to indicate that Marina was in any kind of trouble. She was relieved, to say the least.

"My mind is made up, I can't stand a woman who cheats on me."

"George, Let..."

"No," George screamed, an angry pitch to his voice.

Mrs Magezi jumped. She looked at George and the look in his eyes frightened her.

"Aunt," George said more quietly now, "Marina refuses to sleep with me, she refuses to give me a child and now she goes and sleeps with another man! How do you expect me to forgive her?"

Mrs Magezi knew that it would be useless trying to argue with George.

"I'm very upset, Aunt, Marina has wronged me and I intend to..."

Mrs Magezi was getting more frightened by the look in George's eyes and the edge his tone was taking on. But she still tried to dissuade him.

"I can...can explain Marina's behaviour, I mean...about..." Mrs Magezi was fumbling for the right words. She knew she had to come to Marina's rescue or else this man was going to harm her.

"You mean you can explain why she refuses to have a child with me? Or is she barren? Maybe you knew this all along and you decided to keep quiet." George's eyes narrowed, causing fine wrinkles to form on his forehead. "Did you imagine you'd get away with it?" he continued menacingly. "And now you are afraid to face the consequences? Or do you simply want to exonerate yourself from blame?"

"She is not barren, she already has a child," Mrs Magezi blurted out before she could stop herself.

"She has what?" George asked in shocked disbelief. He took a step towards Mrs Magezi and she backed away from him.

"Well...I mean..." She groped for what to say, but the cold look in George's eyes stopped her. He was like a wild elephant gone amok.

"I demand an explanation for this," George said in a dangerously quiet tone.

Mrs Magezi stared at him with exasperation, her eyes pleading with him to understand.

"Well, do you want me to force the truth out of you?"

"Sit down George," Mrs Magezi said. There was no backing out now. "You know very well that Marina is an orphan," she began. She looked at George as if asking him for permission to continue but he stared back at her indignantly, saying nothing.

"After her parents' death," she continued in a quiet tone, "she went to live at the orphanage..."

The story spilled out of her effortlessly as if she had planned to tell it to George this way. The only indication that George was listening was the shift in his eyes and the grunts of surprise and shock, which occasionally escaped him. Otherwise, he did not interrupt her even once.

When she came to the end, George stood up slowly and went to the window. He stared outside at the cold night. After a moment he remarked, "So you kept all these secrets from me ?"

"Yes," Mrs Magezi's voice was barely a whisper, "but now they are secrets no more."

"I guess so," George answered at length. Abruptly, he moved to the door. "I must go," he said rather urgently.

"You are not going to hurt her, are you?" Mrs Magezi's voice was still a whisper.

"Who?" George asked clearly puzzled.

"Marina. It wasn't her fault you know," her eyes were begging and brimming with tears.

George looked at her for a long time, then he moved out of the door into the cold night.

He is going to kill her, was all Mrs Magezi could think of. He is going to kill the poor innocent girl! I must go and warn her, better still, I should call her.

But she did neither of these. She sat rooted to the chair, gazing into empty space, all energy drained out of her. She wished her husband was around to take care of the messy situation.

Chapter Seven

Dee was surprisingly calm. This was real perplexing. He had envisaged this moment for the last four years and he had expected his heart to be beating uncontrollably, when the moment finally came. But here he was, completely drained of all excitement, the excitement which he had thought would come with revenge.

"I will avenge your blood," he remembered the oath he had made when he saw his sister's mangled body, purportedly after the fatal accident. But he knew better for he remembered the face of that man when he had first seen him with his sister.

"What are you doing with that man. He looks..."

"I know what you mean, Dee, but it's only for the money," Lisa had answered confidently and he had believed her.

"Don't let the money blind you and cloud your better reasoning. As they say, money is the best servant, but the worst master."

"What do you mean?" Lisa had asked, laughing.

"Well, a good servant in that it will do everything that you tell it to do, but a bad master because it will make you work like a donkey."

"Advice taken, brother. In fact, I'm thinking of leaving him."

"Do that."

But it had never happened that way. George had apparently caught her cheating on him. Dee had arranged for her to leave the country fearing George's retribution. Lisa came back when they all thought the storm had abated. But George was a man who neither forgot nor forgave. He had murdered her, he had murdered Dee's only sister!

Dee knew he had to get close to George if he was to accomplish what he intended to do. Luckily, George could not remember having seen him with Lisa. Dee pretended to be a car dealer and even invested money in their shoddy deals.

Marina had presented herself as a priceless gift, a perfect weapon to use to take revenge on George. Dee knew she was very unhappy in her marriage to George. She looked like a frightened kitten who needed protection and was starved of love. The rest had been easy. He knew George would find out sooner than later about his affair with his wife. He would then come to get him. Dee would have the perfect reason to kill him, in self defence.

It was a perfect plan, he thought as he sat now waiting for George to come and meet his death. But he was not excited, probably because he realised he could not abandon Marina as had previously been his plan. One of the reasons was that he had fallen deeply in love with her. But there was something else. She is one of us, how can I leave her? he kept on telling himself.

He had found out about her identity the second time he had made love to her. As she lay in his arms, sated, she started lapsing into Kinyarwanda. At first he was shocked, in fact jolted to his roots to hear her talk that language. He did not ask her where she had learnt the language but had instead gone and done some research on her. He found out that she was an orphan just like himself, her parents having perished in the genocide just like his had. But fortunately for him, he had remained with one sister, Lisa, at least for a few years. That's when he knew that he had to include her in his plans of leaving the country after he had disposed of George.

The telephone startled him out of his reverie. He was disoriented as he answered it.

"Dee, it is George, he has had a terrible accident, he is, we..." Marina could not continue. Sobs were raking her body. Dee let her cry for sometime.

"Dee...I..." she tried again.

"Is he dead?" Dee asked quietly.

"No, but he is badly hurt..."

"I will be there in a minute," he said putting down the receiver.

***

George lay in hospital in a deep coma. Anyone who saw the mangled car could not believe that anyone could have come out of it alive. His legs were severely lacerated, but for the time being, they were just bandaged and were being supported by wooden splints.

Marina, Dee and the Magezis all kept vigil at the hospital. Nobody said much, each seemed to be engrossed in their own thoughts. Dee, as usual kept to himself, talking only when talked to. Marina was consumed by guilt about what she had been about to do. The phone to tell her of George's accident had rung as she was getting out of the house. Yet she took no responsibility for what had happened to George. She knew that night he could have killed her.

On the third day, the neuro-surgeon made his weekly round. The doctors, interns and nurses who accompanied him seemed to hold him in great awe. He ordered everyone out of the private room where George lay, leaving only the entourage which had accompanied him.

"Why is he being treated like a small god?" Mrs Magezi asked the moment they were in the corridor.

"Because he is the 'god' around here, ma'am," Dee replied cynically.

"Why is that?" she asked again.

"Well, because he is the only trained neuro-surgeon this country has."

"Oh, man," Mr Magezi sighed. "I hope no one ever gets a silly idea and decides to put a bullet through his brainy head because then the whole country would be sunk."

"Yes," Dee answered. "I hope not."

The door to the room opened and the medical team filed out. One intern beckoned to Dee. "We are taking him for some X-rays," he explained. "We should be back shortly."

"Right," Dee answered. He went and informed the small group of what the intern had told him. They went back inside the room and watched while George, strapped to a stretcher, was wheeled out. They settled down to wait.

Two hours later, he was wheeled back by two nurses. They looked at them anxiously before Mr Magezi asked one of them, "What is wrong with him?"

The nurse shook her head. "The professor will have to read these first," she said holding out the films for them to see.

"You mean...the...surgeon...something?"

"The neuro-surgeon, yes. He is also a professor."

"And when will that be?" Mr Magezi asked.

"Tomorrow, or the day after," she answered

"Is there anything we can do now?" Mr Magezi asked again.

"Yes," the nurse answered impatiently. "Just wait."

163

The following day, the professor came back. He scanned the films professionally before saying anything.

"Are you his wife?" he asked turning to Marina.

"Yes," Mr Magezi replied before she could say anything. "And I'm his uncle and these...are well...we are all family," he said his hand sweeping over his wife and Dee.

The professor regarded him quietly then said, "George suffered two fractures on both his thighs and as a result bled profusely. The excessive loss of blood sent him into shock and that is why he is in a coma." He glanced at them briefly before continuing, "But there is something else. As you know, there is a lot of fat in bones and when he injured his thigh bones, some fat, which we call emboly in medical terms, escaped into his blood system and caused a blockage of oxygen to the tissues. This blockage could easily spread to the lungs, so we have to try and dislodge the fat. Are you following?" he asked them.

"Yes," Mr Magezi answered quietly.

"We can only dislodge the fat by feeding him plenty of fluids through this," the professor said, pointing to the nasogastric tube which had been inserted in George's nostril.

The room fell silent. The professor looked around then asked, "Is there any question?"

"Ah...yes," Mr Magezi answered. "What are his chances?"

The professor's face was expressionless as he answered, "The mortality of such patients is up to ninety percent."

"And...isn't there anything...something we can do?" Mrs Magezi asked, tears forming in her eyes.

"I'm afraid not. What remains now is between him and his God."

***

Two weeks passed and still there was no change in George's health.

The Magezis had stopped spending the nights at the hospital because Mrs Magezi was not feeling well. But Dee religiously came and spent the night with Marina.

George's parents had long been summoned from the Sese Islands but only his mother had come. His father had apparently disowned his son after the latter had refused to send him money regularly.

Marina could now afford to go home and rest and leave the patient in his mother's care. On such occasions, Dee always drove her home and picked her up to take her back to the hospital.

They had never mentioned their aborted elopement. But Marina knew it was time to get it out of the air and make herself clear to Dee, once and for all.

So one day, when Dee was driving her from the hospital, she asked him, "Dee, where had you planned for us to go that night?"

He turned and looked at her before answering. "To France," he answered mildly.

"Why France? And where would you get all the money for the air tickets?"

"You ask too many questions but for your first question, because I have many friends in that country and I speak perfect French, and so do you," he added with a flicker in his eyes. "And as for the money, do I look like a poor person to you or do you think I make stones where I work? No, baby, I make money." He made as if to draw her closer and hug her but Marina gently pushed him away.

"What is it, baby, don't you love me any more?" He said it carelessly but Marina knew he was serious.

"I don't think I ever loved you, Dee," she answered quietly. "I was just..." she struggled for the right word, "...enchanted, by your charm."

Dee did not respond immediately. "I see," he sighed. "Funny," he continued in his lazy drawl, "all along I thought you were in love with me, as I was with you." He turned his big brown eyes on her and this time they were not laughing. "Marina, is this the way you play with people's hearts?" he asked quietly.

Marina felt something turn inside her. But she did not want to get into an emotional argument now. So much was weighing down on her mind. The effort it took to nurse George, the disturbing news she had received from Hoima that Father Marcel was weaker than ever before and had asked to see her. She knew she had to go to him.

"I don't think there was anything deep between us, Dee." she said carefully. "I think we both got carried away," she added, forcing the words out of her mouth, not believing them herself. But knowing it was the right thing to do.

A clean get away from Dee was all she wanted now. She had to push those wonderful memories to the back of her mind and pretend they never happened. She did not need the kind of person like Dee now. Young, romantic, and insecure. Yes, she could tell that Dee was a very insecure person, and maybe he needed her more than she needed him. Yet she needed a mature, dependable person, one who would offer her a shoulder to cry on.

"What time do you want me to pick you up?" he asked breaking into her thoughts when they finally reached her house.

"Dee, honestly, you don't have to do this. I can-" she began to say but Dee cut her off with an authoritative voice.

"Ten?"

"Okay," she answered reluctantly.

"I will be here," he answered before he drove off.

Chapter Eight

Two months of sleepless nights and anxiety at the hospital had finally taken their toll on them. Dee had long disappeared from the scene and no one seemed to know where he was. Mrs Magezi could not come anymore because she was not feeling well, nor could her husband who was extremely busy at his law office. George's mother had long gone back to the islands because her husband had threatened to chase her if she stayed another week.

George had regained consciousness but at times, Marina wished he had remained unconscious. He was now more demanding, irritable and in much pain; maybe he suffered from more of the psychological than physical pain. The professor had told them that the injured legs had been attacked by a severe infection which could not be controlled by drugs and he had no option but to amputate both legs.

At other times, George was very unreasonable and he would scream at her at the slightest mistake and call her derogatory names. Mrs Magezi was her only comfort then, always reminding her that it was still her duty as his wife to nurse her husband despite what had transpired between them. Marina now missed the old lady's wise words of encouragement and unreserved kindness to take her through the day. Her only source of comfort now were tears.

One morning, Mr Magezi appeared. He looked haggard and withered.

"What is it ?" Marina asked, rushing to him.

He did not answer but went to the only chair in the room and sank into it. George had dozed off and had pulled up the blanket which now covered the whole of his head.

"How is he?" Mr Magezi asked dropping his voice to a whisper.

Marina shrugged but said nothing.

"Your Aunt is very sick," he said after a moment. "She has been admitted here in this hospital. She had a stroke and...the doctors...fear that her left side could be paralysed...permanently."

"A stroke?" Marina asked, shocked. "But I...never knew that...that."

"I know, Marina. Your Aunt never, or rather we preferred to keep it a secret. But she has always suffered from high blood pressure. I'm sorry, we should have told you."

Marina went to him and took his hands in hers. "It's all right. I will be right there. What ward is she in?" she asked him.

He told her and they left together.

Marina found Mrs Magezi in a private room. She was conscious but her breathing was laboured. She was being aided by an oxygen mask to breathe. Marina sat by her bed and held her hands. The sick woman held on to her tightly and Marina saw the tears which came into her eyes.

"You will be alright, Aunt," Marina whispered in her ear. They stayed like that until the latter fell asleep.

"I will be back to help you at night," she told Mr Magezi before she left to go and attend to her husband's needs.

***

Marina soon fell into that routine. Popping in to give Mr Magezi a hand and at the same time attending to George's needs. She would be up the whole night, and even during the day she could not rest. George was becoming more difficult. Every time she went to check on Mrs Magezi; he would accuse her of being with her boyfriend.

"Your hot little pussy cannot let you sit down even for a while, can it? Every time you have to look for a man to dip his thing in it. Go ahead , after all, you used to give it to other men even when I was still man enough. And to think that at fifteen you were already 'eating' things. Then you come and pretend with me that you don't want to go to bed with me. Women! The only time you can claim she is yours is when you are holding her in your arms."

Marina was saved by the fact that he could not walk otherwise he would have hit her. But on such occasions, she simply ignored him and went off to nurse Mrs Magezi. When she came back, he would refuse to talk to her for hours and even refuse her from touching him 'with the semen of another man on her hands'.

His friends rarely came to see him, and when they did, he spent time telling them about her infidelity, or accusing them of robbing him blind, now that he could not monitor his businesses.

"You don't have to go through this, it will soon weigh you down," Mr Magezi told her one day.

"Do I have an option?" Marina asked.

"Of course you do. For one , you don't have to spend the whole night by your Aunt's bed, and secondly, you don't have to put up with what George is putting you through. He is such a selfish person!"

Marina kept quiet. She wondered if his wife had told him the whole story leading to George's accident and how George blamed his wife for it.

"I'm doing what I have to do," she answered wearily.

"I have sent for our daughter and until she comes, I want you to take a break from all this, okay?" he smiled at her reassuringly and Marina smiled back and assured him that she would do as he had asked.

***

On the morning of the twelfth of June, Mrs Magezi passed away quietly in her sleep. Marina was still sleeping when Mr Magezi came to tell them, crying hysterically. George, who had spent a particularly bad night due to the gnawing pain from the stumps was still awake.

"She is gone," Mr Magezi sobbed. "She is gone...gone..."

"Isn't she lucky?" George said, looking at Mr Magezi with disgust. "She doesn't have to suffer any more."

Mr Magezi stopped sobbing and stared at him. "Are you talking to me?" he asked in confusion.

"Sure," George answered lightly. "I'm talking about your dead wife and wondering how, at times, God can be so unfair. He should have let her suffer a little more, say for another year."

Marina, who had been awakened by Mr Magezi's sobbing, looked at her husband incredulously but he ignored her and continued mercilessly, "I hope all Satan's angels are waiting for her at hell's gates."

"Why...does...he say...that?" Mr Magezi asked, turning to Marina.

"Forget it," Marina said soothingly, leading him out of the room.

George looked at them as they went out. That terrible day of the accident came back to him with full force. He remembered leaving the Magezi's residence, boiling with anger, his only intent to punish Marina. Then the crash into an electric pole, and the car overturning, then falling deep into a ditch.

From there, he did not remember anything else. If it had not been for what she had told him about Marina, the accident would not have happened. He would still be a man! Why had she not told him the whole story before?

***

It was Marina, with the help of other Magezi relatives who saw to the arrangements to transport the casket to the village for burial. Mr Magezi broke down completely and could not handle anything. Marina also saw to informing their daughter in America.

After the burial, Mr Magezi came back to the city. Their daughter could not stay for long and soon he was left all by himself. Their 'daughter' indeed! She could now understand Mr Magezi's sense of helplessness. But what she could not understand was how (and why) her Aunt had successfully managed to keep this 'mega' secret from her, and all the other friends the family associated with. No one had ever talked about it, as far as Marina could remember.

She remembered the times she had brought up the issue of their daughter: why she never visited or sent them pictures, or called; and how it would always be her Aunt who answered with suitable answers.

The shock of eventually seeing their 'daughter' as a white - well, almost a white person, if one took away the kinky black hair, had still not worn off.

"It's a long story, Marina," Mr Magezi had simply said to her unasked questions. "But one day I will explain." And she had left it at that.

Marina put aside her own problems and resorted to catering for the needs of the heart-broken widower. She spent the day with him, preparing his lunch and did not leave until he finished the food on his plate. Then she would go back to hospital to attend to George.

"Where do you get all this strength?" he often asked her. "At times, I think you have an extra ton of energy stashed away somewhere. Stop pampering me like a baby and concentrate on your own patient."

Marina would only smile. She knew he needed her terribly and he was only being polite. And as for George, he rarely talked to her these days, and her being there or not, this did not seem to make a difference to him.

Even when she told him that she had to go to Hoima briefly because of the urgent summons she had received that Father Marcel was probably no more, he had just stared at her and sneered saying that she was going to check on her long-time boyfriend.

Sometimes Marina pitied him. He was so much eaten up with jealousy, pain and frustration that everything else around him was inconsequential. The stumps were giving him problems again and the doctor had said that he might have to undergo another operation.

George would not hear of it. He was sick and tired of the hospital where he had spent close to six months now. He wanted to be flown to America where he would have better treatment.

"I understand how you must be feeling, George," Marina tried to reason with him, "but I have to go to Hoima for probably a day or two, and when I come back, we shall see what to do."

He flatly refused to understand. He told her that if she 'disobeyed' him and went to Hoima, he would commit suicide. But Marina knew what she had to do. The following day she left for Hoima.

The first person she met was Stella Maris, and one look at her told her that all was not well.

"He passed away. Just this morning," Stella Maris cried before Marina could ask. The whole parish seemed to be wailing. There were cries from every corner: from the hospital, the convent, the orphanage, the small house where the homeless now lived. Matayo, too was crying hysterically. Surprisingly, Marina could not find tears in her head to shed. She believed that the old prelate had accomplished his mission in this world. Besides, she knew he was at peace with his maker.

Father Marcel was laid to rest the following day at the church's cemetry, where he had asked to be buried. It was a loss which the population at the parish would have to live with. Sister Bernadette was too weak to come to the grave site of her most trusted confidant. It was obvious that she didn't have much longer to live herself.

After the burial, Matayo sought out Marina. She was surprised that she no longer felt anything towards him. Not anger, nor hatred. Time had healed her wounds. She had simply wanted to ignore him.

"There is something I have to discuss with you," he started, obviously ill at ease in her company.

Marina kept quiet and waited.

"It's...it has to do with Father Marcel," he continued, glancing at her before continuing. Still, Marina did not say anything.

"Well, as you know, he so much wanted to see you before he died. Actually, on the morning he died, he called me and made me promise that I would tell you, personally, about his desire to see you." Matayo fell silent. He seemed unsure whether to continue or not. But after a while he continued, "I...I...thought he wanted to find out from you about Rosaria's father. I...I panicked and told him...the truth."

Marina still refused to say anything. What was there for her to say. She wanted to ask if he had asked for his forgiveness, but she let it pass.

"But it wasn't what he had wanted to know," Matayo was talking again. "He wanted to give you something. This," he added, pulling out of his pocket a piece of paper, which had gone yellow with age.

He handed it to Marina and she took it. It was some kind of document. She read through it quickly, noting the day it was written: the 3rd of September of the year Rosaria was born!

Marina closed her eyes, and that's when the tears came. Strong emotions swept through her. She did not want Matayo to see her crying. She excused herself and left him where he was standing.

She was not even sure she wanted to stay at the parish one more minute. She wanted to leave now, leaving behind all the memories, buried where they belonged. They did not belong with her: they had no space in the new life she intended to forge, the sad and sweet memories, friends and foes, the people she had trusted and loved, and those who had betrayed her.

Yet there was one memory, far too strong for her to erase. And one person whom she could not, had no wish to leave behind. She looked again at the document; it was a will. Father Marcel had left all his earthly possessions to Rosaria. She would now be able to take her daughter with her. And begin catering for her like all mothers did for their daughters. And to love her.

***

As she went back to the city the following morning, she had a premonition that something bad had happened. After depositing Rosaria at Mr Magezi's house, she went to the hospital. She was half surprised to find George gone. The nurses told her that he had insisted on being taken back home. When she went home, he did not ask her about her trip and she did not bother to tell him about Father Marcel's death.

But she had something to tell him which could not wait for another day.

The trip to Hoima, and the death of Father Marcel had given her the space and the courage she needed to take the decision. It was high time she began taking her life in her own hands.

172

"I'm leaving you, George," she said to him.

There was no indication that he had heard her.

"There is no need for us to pretend any more. It will do both of us good if we lived under separate roofs," Marina continued.

"Don't even think of getting a coin from me," George said, almost screaming. "You..."

"I won't, George, I don't need your money. Besides..."

"Then go!" he shouted. "Take all your belongings and never..."

"No George, they are your belongings; you bought them...I want to..."

"Women! You are all the same. You are like buses; whoever has money is the one who gets on, when the money is finished, he gets off, and another one gets on!" he spat out.

Marina stared at him. She wanted to cry. She had heard from his friends how he had lost most of his money, and how he had been selling off most of his assets, most of which Marina had not known he possessed. He wanted to raise enough money to take him out of the country. He had even mortgaged their house - his house, to be exact.

But that was not the reason she was leaving him. She was leaving him because she shouldn't have got married to him in the first place...it was a mistake. Yes, everything had been a mistake from the beginning...her parents shouldn't have been killed, Matayo shouldn't have raped her...George should have been told the truth, even she and Dee were a mistake too...

God, she was crying! Quickly, before she could burst into uncontrollable tears, she rushed from the house.

EPILOGUE

Marina and her husband were reclining in the comfortable settee, her legs curled up, and her head resting on his lap. Rosaria was sprawled on the carpeted floor, having fallen asleep after watching her favourite comedy on television.

All was quiet in the sitting room. Marina looked down at Rosaria and for a moment wondered if she had mothered this beautiful girl. After the love I discovered for my daughter, no one can ever take her away from me again except God, she thought to herself.

"She is a lovely child," her husband remarked softly, following his wife's gaze.

"Yes, she is," she agreed. Suddenly, she felt hot tears sting her eyes.

Why am I crying, she asked herself, unable to control the tears flowing down her cheeks in torrents.

"What is it, love?" her husband asked, alarmed.

Too much has happened in my life in such a short time, and I don't know what I could have done without you, she wanted to tell her husband but did not. The tears continued to flow; she had no will to stop them.

She was again thinking of those first days after her first husband's death. George had committed suicide a few weeks after she had left him. His friends and relatives had attributed it to her having left him, but she knew that George could not survive without money.

Dee had later written her a detailed letter:

Too bad that I had to leave [for France] without you. I will always love and cherish you. I already miss you like a child misses its mother. I'm sorry about your husband...

He had gone on to explain everything, attaching all sorts of evidence concerning her late husband which showed what kind of man he had been: a murderer, a thief, a monster. He had offered to marry her, and to

174

adopt Rosaria and give them both a fresh start in France. But Marina had declined the offer, she had also refused to have anything to do with her late husband's wealth, or what little had remained of it, which to her, was blood-stained. her father-in-law had gladly taken over everything, without any shame. After he had disowned his son for not sending him money, and summoned his wife from his sick bed, who could have imagined that he would want to have anything to do with his son's property?

She now remembered when Mr Magezi had first suggested that they could actually get married. At that time, she had thought he was joking. But in the end, she had seen the logic of it all. They both needed each other and she had accepted to become Mrs Magezi.

Now, without warning, she felt an overwhelming urge to ask him about that 'very long story' he had promised to tell her. She knew how painful it was for him, but she needed to know *now*.

"I know, love. It's only fair that you brought this up, and I should have explained long ago, like I promised," he answered when Marina put the question to him.

"Your late Aunt could not conceive for about five years after we had been married," he began. "So I decided to send her to these 'powerful' doctors in America. A few months after she had come back, she 'conceived' and later gave birth to Kimuli, 'our daughter'. You know the rest. We both decided that the best thing to do was to send Kimuli back to America to her father when she was still a baby."

Marina was quiet for a long time. "Did you forgive her?" she asked at length.

"I did. But as it turned out, we could not have a sexual life," her husband answered quietly.

"Why? Which means you never forgave her!"

"No, not because of that Marina. You see, I was...the one to blame. I...I am not...was not man enough." He was speaking with a lot of difficulty. "We went to see a doctor after she failed to conceive again and it was discovered that my sperm count was - is very low, meaning that I could not...will never be able to father children."

Marina drew him in her arms and held him tightly, wishing to take way the pain she knew he was feeling and must have felt then.

"But what about now?" she whispered to him. "With this new technology, we could try-I mean it's not too late!"

"I know, love. But I have Rosaria and you. What more could a man ask for?"

175

GLOSSARY

abaami - kings
abanzi - enemies
abaswa - people of low class or who are uncultured, uncouth
bahutu/hutu - plural
batutsi/tutsi - plural
inyenzi - cockroach
inyenzikazi - female cockroach
interahamwe - people who plan, agree and attack together
mabuja - addressing a lady one highly respects, like a maid addressing
      or referring to her mistress
maguru ya sarwaya - legs of an ostrich
muhutu - singular
mututsi - singular
mvunamuheto - a swear word, curse or abusive reference to a person
      for being stupid - figuratively
mwamikazi - princess or queen
nyakubahwa - honourable